20/20

Perfect Vision or Political Pipe Dream?

BILL HUGHES

This book was printed in the United States of America
by Gorham Printing, Centralia, Washington

To order additional copies of this book, contact:
    Bill Hughes
    1204 NE 65th Street
    Vancouver, WA 98665
    (360) 694-7352
    BHughes803@aol.com

Dedicated to my late loving wife Winnie.

PROLOGUE

I suppose, at some time in his or her life, everyone has made the remark: "I could write a book" or "I should write a book." Having travel and politics as my top avocations, I have attempted to blend the two into this volume. Therefore, the portions relating to travel in Russia are true while the politics that either take place during, or are referred to; between the year 2000 and 2020 are naturally mostly fiction. As stand-up comedy is another one of my avocations, I have interjected a political blurb at the conclusion of some chapters, many of which would be humorous if they weren't so tragic. As in the days of ancient Greek Theater, they contain both comedy and tragedy.

CHAPTER 1

September 27, 2020, was a dark and gloomy day at the Resurrection Retirement Resort as Nurse Lillian Tate made her hourly rounds. It seemed the only way she could break up the monotony of her job was to make up songs in her head that always ended each verse with borrrrring!

She was pleased with her job as it paid well and the perks were better than most. A lot of applicants had tried for the nursing positions at this new facility with its latest nuances in assisted health care. Actually she had grown quite fond of many of the patients and grieved with the passing of every one. The resort offered a different approach to the care of the elderly as well as those with disabilities that precluded them from independent living. This resort featured a petting zoo for those who were ambulatory and, would you believe, a well-stocked fish pond where old fishermen never died, they just exited with a smile on their face. It was soon learned that some of the lady residents were more ardent fisher-persons than many of the men.

Among Lil's patients was a rather unusual chap by the name of Hugh Williams. He had been there since the inception of Resurrection and all she knew about him was what she had been told. It seems he had been the victim of a skiing accident about twenty years ago and had been in a coma ever since. It was rumored he held the modern day record for the comatose state and was sometimes laughingly compared to Rip Van Winkle.

Among other chores, it was one of Lil's responsibilities to check in on Mr. Williams at least two or three times each shift.

There was little or nothing to do for him but to merely check to see that his feeding tube was functioning, take care of his personal hygiene and every other hour, with the aid of an orderly, turn her unconscious patient on his bed.

On this particular day, Lillian Tate arrived a few moments early, dressed in her attractive blue uniform not really looking forward to another daily grind. Lil had become one of the patients' favorites as, ever since the nursing profession became more lenient in its dress code, she wore a different color every day. Indeed, the patients grew to depend on her as their calendar for each working day had its special color. One patient even kidded and remarked that "many, many years ago, due to a popular movie, folks used to say, 'If it's Tuesday, it must be Belgium' and now we say: 'If it's turquoise, it must be Thursday.'"

Before the start of her shift, Lil glanced into Hugh's room and, to her astonishment, saw what she thought was a small, but very discernible movement. She got on the phone and immediately summoned the head nurse, who in turn called a physician who responded in a heartbeat. Armed with his stethoscope he rushed into the room and immediately detected an increase in the patient's heart rate over that which was shown on his chart...While bending over Hugh, he noticed that one eye started to twitch and soon neither he nor Lillian could believe he was actually emitting guttural sounds.

By this time, other members of the staff started to gather at Hugh's door and one of them laughingly stated he had dibs on the popcorn concession. What they probably didn't realize was the fact they were witnessing modern medical history being made right before their eyes.

Fortunately the attending physician had the good common sense to darken the patient's room for he knew if Hugh opened his eyes, after twenty years, he could be blinded. The doctor had seen many news blurbs about our astronauts' inability to function immediately after returning from zero gravity and he realized that Hugh Williams might well experience a similar phenomenon.

Word quickly spread throughout the care facility and some of the residents even went to the chapel to offer up a prayer for their 'new friend.' Rumors were rampant but only a few members of the staff were allowed into 'Rip Van Winkle's' room. As everyone, especially the medical staff, had hoped, very, very slowly, but inexorably, Hugh's muscles began to respond to what must have been a modern miracle.

Within an hour, in the darkened room, the patient's eyelids began to flicker and eventually open. What must have been going through Hugh's head as he felt his eyes were open, but still there was nothing but darkness? Slowly, his vision started to clear and he was able to make out the dimmest of night-lights and soon he was able to observe dark figures around his bed. A few minutes earlier, he had heard conversations but, as this whole episode was not unlike a normal dream, he had not given it much thought.

By this time, the staff of the rest home had summoned one of the most qualified neurologists in the area who jumped at the chance to be probably the first to converse with a man whom had slept for twenty years. He had dealt with many amnesia patients, but to actually interview someone that had been unconscious for two decades might be worthy of a paragraph or two in the medical journals.

On his way to Resurrection Retirement Resort, so many questions raced through his mind. Would he need the expertise of a psychiatrist, as was the case with so many of his patients? Would the patient be cognizant of the fact he had been comatose for twenty years? What would Mr. Williams reactions be when he learned he had been a vegetable for such a long time?

Assuming his mind was still functioning as it had at the time of his accident, what would be his first words? Probably he would inquire about his family first and then there would be many more questions that would demand answers in order to bring him up to speed. It had been said that mankind learns twice as much in every decade as in the previous one and Hugh Williams was twenty years behind.

When Les Laurel, the neurologist, arrived at the care facility he was like a kid with a new toy. He was unable to conceal his joy when he first laid eyes on Hugh for, at first blush; he appeared almost entirely normal. It was an effort for Mr. Williams to speak and he seemed to tire with each utterance but much to Dr. Laurel's delight, his first few words seemed to make sense. Needless to say, Dr. Laurel was like an anthropologist who had just discovered a live baby dinosaur.

Soon Hugh Williams was talking in sentences and was firing questions at the staff like a machine-gun. Imagine his shock when he was informed it was 2020.

"Oh my God, I've lost twenty years…Where's my family? Are they OK? Who's the president? How's the economy? Did we get into any more stupid wars?"

"Hold it," the staff members would respond; "you've been gone for twenty years and you expect us to bring you up to date in twenty minutes?"

What Williams, and even some of the staff weren't aware of, especially the younger members, was that many of them had nearly as many questions about what life was like in the 'olden times' as Hugh had about conditions in the present. Indeed, some of the candy stripers would find any excuse to visit Hugh Williams for he could recall many things that to them were just words on a page in a history book.

During the rare moments when Lil could sneak a short conversation with her favorite patient, she attempted to bring Hugh up to date on some subjects that were more of a personal nature.

"After your exit from the conscious world, Hugh, your daughter took over like a general and looked after your estate. For years she has planned for the day you'd be coming home and wanted to surprise you by leaving your house exactly as you left it.

"After several months, when it became obvious that you might be absent for an extended period of time she packaged your personal papers, took them home and leased out your house. You will be pleased to learn that the rent more than covered your mortgage payments and your house has been paid off for a number of years. I'm sure your daughter, Kim, will have a lot to tell you when she comes in this afternoon."

Sure enough, when Kim arrived she had a briefcase full of papers. She explained to Lil that they were from Hugh's home office and consisted of mostly the periodicals Hugh had subscribed to at the time of his accident. She then displayed copies of publications such as Human Events and reports from the National Taxpayer's Union that all carried dates like 1999 and 2000. "I thought this might help Dad transition from his world of twenty years ago to the present", explained Kim. Her supposition was right on target, for when Hugh was able to comprehend and remember some of the incidents of those earlier days, he was able to utilize the information to help put his earlier life into proper context.

FOOD FRIGHT

Feeding children who can't feed themselves. Who could be against a mission like that? The administrators of the federal program intended to do just that. A three-year audit by the U.S. Department of Agriculture has questioned $5.5 million of expenses in a federally subsidized California program that is supposed to reimburse non-profit day-care centers the cost of providing children with two meals and one snack each day. Total expenditures to the California grant operation, the largest among all states, runs nearly $170 million per year. According to the report, the state "fostered a lax environment in which sponsors could personally enrich themselves through questionable or fraudulent schemes which they could perpetuate with little likelihood of detection." It took federal watch dogs, who normally need seeing-eye dogs of their own, to dig up these schemes which included the purchase of a 5,000 square foot home by a day-care providing couple, ski trips, vehicles, clothing and, ironically, tuition for the providers' children. So far, criminal charges have been leveled at 15 people for their attempts to cash-in at the expense of hungry kids...

Capital Ideas
May/June 1999

CHAPTER 2

It appeared that what seemed like every doctor, of every discipline, in the nation came calling for an interview with Hugh Williams. Doctor Laurel decided to use this demand to his advantage. After all, hadn't he already decided to submit this patient to a series of rather exhaustive memory tests? Here was a chance to kill two birds with one stone. The memory tests would reveal whether Mr. Williams suffered any memory loss and those around the complex could glean some history from a man who had lived through many years of it, as Hugh Williams was far from being a young man.

Dr. Laurel was prepared with a battery of questions and wore a wire to record every word of Hugh's response.

"Tell me, Mr. Williams, just how much of your life do you remember?"

"Well, doctor," replied the patient; "my mind seems to get clearer by the minute. My younger years seem like yesterday. It's just a question as to where you want me to begin. I was born in, and received my basic education in, southwestern Iowa, but I'm sure you don't want to be bored with such mundane details."

"No, on the contrary, Mr. Williams, the subject matter is not nearly as important as your ability to recall and relate it. Suppose, however, we commence with any highlights of your past, especially any of those with a historical significance."

"Okay, doctor, why don't I try to recall my travels? I was very fortunate inasmuch as I had traveled rather extensively in my younger days. I had the opportunity to visit all fifty states, at least twice. There are still fifty states, aren't there? . . In addition, I had visited at least forty-six foreign countries. I can recall very vividly, what many folks considered the trip of a lifetime, a trip around the world, including the Trans-Siberian Railway from Moscow to Nakhodka, the commercial port adjacent to Vladivostok."

"And just when did you take that dream trip?" queried Dr. Laurel.

"That particular trip occurred in the summer of 1972" the patient replied.

"Do you mean you undertook such an arduous journey while Russia was still The Soviet Union? Hold those thoughts please, this is too good not to share with any staff members and residents who may be history and geography buffs."

Word quickly spread throughout the resort's campus and indeed, it became necessary to schedule a more or less public interview in the large dining room the next day. Many of the ambulatory patients were anxious to be entertained by something other than instructions in needlepoint or under-water basket weaving. In fact, many felt they may be able to relate to some of Mr. Williams' experiences of some fifty years ago.

Much to Hugh Williams' surprise, when he was taken to the dining room there was standing room only as the interested staff members relinquished as much space as possible to patients in wheel chairs. Upon entering the crowded venue, Hugh jokingly asked;

"Who's minding the store?" His next zinger was "I want the movie rights."

Williams couldn't conceive where so many folks had come from, as, while this was a large institution, all the residents plus the staff for all three shifts couldn't have mustered such a large gathering. What he didn't realize was the fact that many of the employees had kept their school-age children out of school that day for they felt they could learn more about history and geography from this voice from the past than they could possibly learn in one day at school.

Such a packed hall almost demanded there be a PA system and one was quickly hooked up. After a short prayer, delivered by one of the patients, Dr. Laurel introduced Hugh Williams and the crowd burst into a round of applause. When Mr. Williams took the microphone, an eerie silence fell over the room as though the audience was breathlessly waiting to hang onto every word before the first one was uttered. Fortunately one of the staff members had the foresight to tape the 'history lessons' for some of the attendees and especially the youngsters that couldn't take in all the sessions but didn't want to miss a single word.

"Where do I begin? In the early spring of 1972, while employed in the transportation field, I told my boss, Ernie Christensen, that I had reason to believe that I could secure Interstate Commerce authority to operate our trucks between Portland, Oregon and Seattle, Washington. In those days, to operate trucks between and among states, a permit was required from the Interstate Commerce Commission and they were very difficult to come by.

"Ernie looked at me like I had just ridden in on a load of turnips, but hurled this challenge at me. 'I think you're crazy, but if you can pull that off, I'll give you and your wife an all expense paid trip to Europe.' I didn't have the heart to tell him that I had visited Europe a couple of times while in the Merchant Marines, so waited a few days before I came up with a counter-proposal.

"'Chris,' I said, 'I've been to Europe, so if it's all the same with you, I'd like to visit Russia.'

9

'Russia,' he blurted out, 'Why would anyone in his or her right mind want to go to Russia?'

'Well,' I said, you may have answered your own question, but I have always hated communism with a passion and I want to see what makes it work. After all, you were there, weren't you Chris?'

'Yes,' he responded, 'and, take it from me there is nothing there, unless, of course, you like history and hardships. However, I feel I'm on very safe ground regarding those operating rights so if you can pull off that miracle, I'll finance a trip to Russia.'

"I recall that during World War II, America's armed forces had a slogan that said, in effect: 'The difficult we do immediately, the impossible takes a little longer.' Well, needless to say, I wanted to visit the Soviet Union so much I could taste it so I set out to perform the impossible task of obtaining those operating rights. I recall securing about one hundred and fifty shipper witnesses and Chris was so impressed with my testimony on the stand he said; 'Regardless of the outcome, you have already earned the trip. When do you want to leave?' 'Oh, by the way, Chris, did I tell you, that being a railroad buff, all my life I have dreamed of taking a trip on the Trans-Siberian Railroad?'

"'What,' he retorted, 'you mean go all the way to the East Coast of Russia and all the way back?'

'No,' I said, 'when I get to the east Coast, I will take the steamer service to Yokohama, thence to Tokyo where I can make calls for our company. After all, haven't we been hauling containers of malt to the port docks and receiving complaints about the condition of the product upon its arrival in Japan?'

'You know,' he responded, 'Now I see why you're my sales manager, you're the only son of a bitch I know of that can take a trip to Europe and turn it into a trip around the world.'

"At this point, I must ask how many of you are really interested in what Russia was like fifty years ago?"

The response was virtually unanimous.

"Okay, you asked for it, but please be so kind as to interrupt me when and if you get bored or you need a coffee or potty break. Keep in mind you must accept this concept in the time in which it took place. We had many revisionists trying to rewrite history so I can and will relate what actually happened to me.

"Why Russia? The response was almost universal when we informed our relatives and friends that we were going around the world…the hard way, namely through The Soviet Union by auto and the Trans-Siberian Railway. The best explanation I could offer was to the effect that I was tired of condemning anything and everything that smacked of socialism, merely on the basis of someone's opinion instead of getting the knowledge firsthand. This desire, coupled with a nearly lifelong yearning to ride the Trans-Siberian Railway, prompted us to make this trip.

I must say that I began to doubt the wisdom of my trip selection when even our Travel Bureau asked if we realized what we were getting into. It seemed the Intourist tour operator in San Francisco thought we were some kind of nuts. Intourist was the official travel agency of the Soviet Union.

"The paper from the State Department that accompanied our passports didn't help the cause either by warning us against driving in the Soviet Union and the prison terms that are handed out for the infraction of Russian traffic laws. Now this whole ordeal became a challenge and just made me more determined than ever to tackle it. Whatever the State Department said not to do, I did as I felt I would be missing something. This assumption was borne out all across Russia as we watched tour leaders collecting passports from their charges when checking in at hotels while my wife Winnie and I were forced to interact with the local populace.

"Flying over the ice cap to London, I couldn't make myself believe that I was on my way to Russia in spite of the fact I had all my tickets and vouchers in my pocket.

Arriving in London at 10 P.M., my time, and discovering it was 6 A.M. their time, makes one wonder about their biological clock more than what the future may hold in store. After a quick sightseeing tour of London, I made my connection to Copenhagen, where I

Flying over polar ice cap...June 1972

was to meet my wife who had been visiting her daughter in Greece on the Island of Corfu. Sure enough, as the travel bureau people had said, she arrived just one hour after I did.

"We had a lot of talking to do after our two weeks absence from one another and I had put a copy of our local paper in my flight bag to help her catch up on the news. After two days of resting and sightseeing, which included a hydra-foil ride to Malmo, Sweden, we boarded Finnair for the flight to Helsinki. It was during this flight that I happened to read an article in an English language newspaper that informed us that all individual travelers from America had been barred from all points east of the Volga and especially on the Trans-Siberian Railway. The article speculated that this was due to either the troop movements along the Chinese border or the movement of war material for use in North Vietnam. Did you ever see a grown man cry? So near, yet so far!

"We could do nothing but wait until we reached Leningrad and hope. I had made up my mind before leaving home that I would try to be as objective as possible and merely report on what I saw in the Soviet Union without much editorializing. I soon discovered this would be quite a task for we began to form opinions even before we took off from Helsinki. First, our flight on Aeroflot was an hour late in departing. The heat was breaking all records in that area and with the overhead air not working we were very, very uncomfortable. We wondered if that old two-engine prop job could make the fifty-minute trip, but it did.

"The stewardess was rather attractive in her blue uniform and quite polite. She even said please when she announced that there would be no photographs. The controls for the seat-backs did not work and everyone was leaning into the laps of the passengers behind them like dominos. One could feel the wooden frame of the backrest of the seat in front of them pressing against their knees. Shortly after take-off, the stewardess passed out candies followed by oranges and miniature glasses of champagne."

At this point, Mr. Williams hesitated and asked, "Are you sure you want to hear this long dissertation? Aren't you becoming bored?"

The response was again unanimous.

"No, no," they responded almost in unison.

"You make us feel as if we are living the history of about fifty years ago and your narration brings out so much more life than the printed word."

"Well, if you insist," replied Mr. Williams, "but I still think it's *my* turn to start asking you what has transpired during my long 'nap.' Tell you what. I'll supply you with a list of questions and we'll trade answers. I'm sure you won't have all the answers on the tip of your tongue, so I respectfully request that you consult experts in the respective fields so I may get at least a synopsis of what has transpired in various fields during my absence from the human race. Gosh, I feel like a professor assigning homework but don't you think it's a fair trade?"

Those in attendance nodded in agreement and all agreed to bring pens and notepads for the next day's "history session."

BIRD BRAINS

Like the flightless birds from which they came, ostrich and emu meat never took off with American consumers, the way ranchers hoped they would in the 1960s. Guess who may pay for the wild ride?

Currently the U.S. Department of Agriculture (USDA) picks up the tab for inspecting commonly consumed meats like beef, pork, lamb, chicken and turkey. This summer a provision was inserted into a House farm spending bill to add ostrich and emu meat to that list, even though most exotic or specialty food industries would reimburse taxpayers for inspection services at around $38 per hour. Because the meat is easy to overcook, ostrich and emu is primarily served only in fancy restaurants, which is why producers want a little help from their friends in Congress. Strangest of all, the USDA isn't sure that this action will reduce emu and ostrich meat prices for consumers, nor is it certain whether it will need to ask Congress for more money to cover the inspections at some later time.

Big birds aren't the only winners in the farm lottery. This year the House and Senate have also approved $200 million in buyouts for surplus crops such as cranberries and black-eyed peas, along with $100 million to cottonseed producers. Does this nest of market-mauling subsidies seem bird-brained to you?

Capital Ideas
July/August 2000

CHAPTER 3

The next day brought the necessity of finding larger quarters for the Hugh Williams lecture for, as word spread, the audience swelled exponentially. Now, at least for a while, the shoe was to be on the other foot. Mr. Williams felt as if his brain would explode for he had many questions and couldn't wait for the pressure relief that the uttering of these inquiries would bring.

"Are you ready? Pens and note pads in hand? Here is your assignment: At the time of my misfortune, some of the questions uppermost in the minds of the general public were as follows, and please tell what solutions, if any, have come to the forefront in the last twenty years:

1. One of the big arguments during the 2000 elections was education. Some argued that we needed more money for education while others maintained we needed more education for the money. Who won and what transpired?

2. Another big issue was energy and the high cost of fuel. What has happened in that field?

3. Both major political parties at that time tried to outdo each other with social security promises. Is it still solvent?

4. Health care costs had become exorbitant. Was this ever resolved and how?

5. Land use. Private property rights were paramount, but Uncle Sam was taking it away in big chunks. Did common horse sense ever prevail?

6. The so-called Right to Choose. Was this ever repealed?

7. Were our Constitutional rights preserved, especially those under Amendments 1, 2, 5 and 10?

8. Transportation. Do we still have gridlock?

9. Government waste. Did they ever plug the leaks?

10. Welfare. Is it still as prevalent?

11. Jobs—Economy. Has it been boom or bust?

12. Taxes at all levels?

13. Balance of payment in Foreign Trade. Did we achieve it?

14. Foreign Aid. Are we still sending it?

15. Crime and punishment?

16. Immigration?

17. World hunger. Do we still have hungry people around the world?

"These are but a few of the questions circulating in my head. In addition to the answers to the questions I have just presented you with, I'm sure you will have many other items and information on subjects that never even occurred to me. Indeed, if technology advanced, even as much in the last twenty years as it had in the ten years prior to my accident, there are no doubt questions about subjects that weren't even known in my day. Please feel free to volunteer any information, which will assist me in resurrecting the last two decades.

"Since my regaining of consciousness, I have heard repeated references to 9/11 and couldn't help but wonder why an emergency phone number would play such a heavy role in today's society. One of the nurses was kind enough to inform me that it was nine eleven, not the phone number, nine-one-one, but September 11, 2001. It's hard for me to conceive what she told me about the World Trade Center and the

Pentagon and the thousands that perished that day.

"I certainly hope that America didn't respond like Carter and Clinton did when attacked by terrorists."

"No way," interjected a voice from the front row. "Sorry to interrupt, but I was a pioneer in the new department set up by George Bush, known as Homeland Security. My name is Denny Bryant and I have some first-hand information regarding America's response to the terrorists' attacks.

"You may recall, Hugh, that just prior to your skiing tragedy, George W. Bush was declared winner in the presidential election of 2000. Some folks claimed he was a weak sister, a milquetoast and even downright stupid. Well, I'm here to tell you that he was none of the above. True, he had his own novel way of butchering some of the words in our language, but he turned out to be the right man in the right place at the right time.

"What some of the folks at this gathering might not be aware of is the fact that then President Bush decided to fight fire with fire. We will probably never know whether Mr. Bush had a hand in it, but it came to pass that many of the leaders of the terrorists started showing up missing. Many folks still believe that somebody in the State Department, White House, whatever, employed members of the mafia and contracts were put out on our enemies.

"This started showing up in about 2003 not too long after a deck of cards was printed with each card depicting a photo of our most wanted in the Arab world. We had high hopes that the United Nations would help us to establish a new government in such places as Afghanistan, Iraq, Iran and the whole middle-east. They proved again that they were the gutless wonder and Uncle Sam had to carry the largest burden with lots of help from Great Britain.

"It took a few years, but slowly and surely, the folks in the Middle East came to realize they would have a much higher standard of living under a democratically elected free government. Wiping out religious taboos and superstitions that had governed their lives for about 1,400 years couldn't be accomplished overnight. It finally came to pass that the majority of the United Nations wised up but it took terrorists attacks in nations all over to world to make them see the light. America was finally able to bring home some of her 'world police force' and now peace reigns supreme."

"Thanks, Denny. That's pretty good for the lead-off batter. What a good example of what I had in mind for our information exchange. As I have given you enough assignments to last a full semester and I am just a little weary, suppose we dismiss the class a little early this session to enable some of you to research my long wish list."

BRUISE SHIP

Pigs may not be able to fly but they sure can swim. Weighing in at 72,000 gross tons the two cruise liners presently being built in Pascagoula, MS will be the first of their kind to wallow out of a U.S. shipyard in more than forty years. And guess who's already underwritten the tickets for the first voyage? Hint: the word begins with "tax" and ends with "payer". Thanks to a loan guarantee of $1.1 billion from the U.S. Maritime Administration, the Shipbuilding Company known as American Classic Voyages, will sink or swim on the backs of hard-working Americans. And most bets are on sink: after all, borrowers defaulted on $2.4 billion of Maritime Administration Loans for other tubs in the 1980s. What's more Congress continues to play dreamboat to bloated maritime unions and their demands making more efficient foreign carriers attractive to those who can't afford to pay the overhead on U.S.flagged ships.

Although the new ships are being built in Senate Majority Trent Lott's (R-MS) home state, this floating oinker is a bipartisan brainchild. The venture's second biggest backer is Hawaii's Democrat Senator Dan Inouye, who's ready to hand American Classic a monopoly on the continental U.S.-Hawaii cruise route.

Capital Ideas
July/August 1999

CHAPTER 4

The next morning found Hugh wondering if he had scared away his audience as he made his way to the 'classroom' but his fears were soon dispelled as he entered the venue that had standing room only.

"Good morning class, are we all ready for your first day in the USSR?" Not even waiting for the unanimous answer, Hugh launched into his belated travelogue.

"Upon arrival in Leningrad, we couldn't help but observe that most of the plane servicing was done by women. We were forced to remain on board for what seemed like an eternity and later learned that the entire passenger list was checked before anyone was allowed to deplane. Again the terrific heat contributed to our discomfort but we could not blame this on the Russians.

"When the loading ramp was pulled up to the plane and we were finally allowed to exit, I'm sure I looked a little ridiculous wearing my Finnish straw hat in the wind and the rain. At the foot of the gangway stood a Russian soldier with a rifle and an expression on his face that did not exactly say welcome. As I emerged from the plane, the wind caught my hat and blew it into a puddle of water under the wing. I took a long look at the soldier and then at the hat trying to determine if I should retrieve it. I casually walked over and picked it up and the soldier just stood there, devoid of any expression.

"The passengers were herded into a rather small room where we were confronted with the Immigration officials. They sat in tiny cubicles next to a series of iron gates. Talk about cold fish, I will never forget the way they looked us over while checking our travel documents and removing the first portion of our Russian visas. When they were satisfied that our papers were in order, they opened an iron gate to let us pass. I can vividly recall the clanking thud of the gate closing behind us. Thoughts of the 'Iron Curtain' crossed my mind and I must say that at this point, I began to have second thoughts about the wisdom of our 'adventure.' With the echo of the sickening clank still in my ears, I was confronted by a forty-foot high portrait of Lenin… All I could think of was…son of a bitch, people are literally dying to escape this place and we actually paid good money to get in.

"We noticed the other passengers were filling out forms and decided that perhaps we should be doing the same. When I finally found one printed in English, we proceeded to answer the questions, which pertained mostly to the amount of cash we carried and in which currency. They also wanted information as to printed matter as well as jewelry and other valuables. We declared only our money and didn't realize until later we should have listed such items as cameras, radios and the like. As it turned out, this was probably a wise move as we later learned that it was against the law to bring a tape recorder into the Soviet Union and they frowned on tourists from the West with movie cameras.

"Next came the mad scramble for baggage. I couldn't believe that a city the size of Leningrad could have such an antiquated airport with such primitive-baggage-handling procedures. Shortly after we landed, it seemed that a tour group arrived from London and it was every man for himself trying to claim one's luggage as it appeared on a belt through a little hole in the wall. Can you imagine approximately three hundred people in a room about twenty by forty trying to fight their way through wall-to-wall people while loaded down with way-too-much baggage? I fully expected to see people passing out from the stifling heat and humidity.

"Struggling under the weight of four suitcases, two loaded flight bags, a large camera case filled to the brim with film plus a purse that must have weighed forty pounds, we somehow made our way to the customs line where most of the passengers were really getting a thorough search. The customs men left very little untouched as they searched the baggage of everyone in front of us. I felt sorry for some of the ladies who had their purses turned upside down and the contents spilling all over the counter and floor. They seemed especially interested in printed matter looking over every article in magazines and books. It was then I remembered I had a copy of the Vancouver, Washington *Columbian* sticking right out of the pocket of my flight bag.

"I was prepared to surrender the paper, but to our amazement, we were waved on through with a courteous smile. I'll always think that perhaps Dan Evans, governor of Washington at that time, must have put a good word in for us as I had seen him in a hometown jewelry store just prior to my departure from the states. I had informed him of our impending trip and, as he had just returned from the Soviet Union, he recommended some points of interest.

"However, I did feel just a twinge of disappointment of not having an encounter with customs but upon second thought, perhaps it was for the best as I am sure if we had been searched as thoroughly as the others, upon discovery of my slide camera, still camera, movie camera, binoculars, transistor radio and cassette-tape recorder, I would have had a difficult time convincing the Russians we were not members of the CIA.

"Leaving the customs room, we found ourselves in a lobby with several sets of double doors leading to the street. Much to our surprise, only one half of one door was open in spite of the fact that hundreds of people were trying to get in and out with their luggage. After fighting our way through this small opening, we found ourselves standing out in the rain not knowing where to go and wondering why we hadn't been met by Intourist as scheduled. It was at this time we discovered what was to be our biggest handicap in Russia, namely the language barrier. Absolutely nobody around could speak English and as my Russian vocabulary consisted of *nyet* and *da*, I had no choice but to make my way back into the customs section ignoring the "Do Not Enter" signs written in plain English on the doors.

"The customs man gave us directions to Intourist, but I must have misunderstood as we soon found ourselves in a restricted area on the edge of the airfield. The looks of the policemen and soldiers told me I was lost so back we went to the customs for more explicit instructions. The Intourist office was located in the departure area and we would have to elbow our way through thousands of people to reach it. Strange, but all the destinations posted at the windows at the head of each line were cities such as East Berlin, Prague, Warsaw, etc. No Western cities…I wondered why, no, only kidding. You would have had to live in that era and under those paranoid conditions to appreciate the humor of that remark. Using the same manners, or lack thereof, as *they* displayed, I pushed and shoved until I succeeded in reaching what seemed like an impossible destination.

"The office turned out to be not much larger than a cubbyhole and again using my newly learned Russian manners, I marched right up to the desk, ignoring the twenty-odd people that were probably awaiting their turn. The desk was manned by a rather attractive blonde but, much to my dismay, she spoke only Russian and French. Fortunately a girl had overheard my attempt to communicate and asked if she might be of assistance. At this point, I was so happy to hear English I could have kissed her. I showed her our vouchers and she conveyed the information to the lady behind the desk. Whether that lady realized that Intourist had goofed or whether she was just trying to he a good hostess, I'll never know, but she dropped everything and indicated I should follow her. She went through that milling mob like a Green Bay Packer and I was hard pressed to keep up with her. I had left my wife Winnie standing on the street guarding our luggage and upon our arrival back to where she was patiently waiting, our newly found friend barked an order to men parked in autos across the street. They nearly fought over who was going to have the honor of driving us into the city of Leningrad."

With that, Hugh Williams had to admit that he was thoroughly exhausted and announced that it was time to call it a day.

"I certainly hope some of you will have some information for me tomorrow on at least one of the subjects I outlined previously. Keep in mind I am just as curious about the last twenty years as I hope you are about the previous decades, and our adventures in Soviet Russia."

SCAMTRACK

If you're ever in Oklahoma City, OK, bound for Ft Worth, TX, do your fellow passengers a favor. Tear up your train ticket and call a limousine—it's cheaper.

The State of Oklahoma has contracted with Amtrak, the federally run passenger railroad, to provide service between Oklahoma City and Ft Worth for a fare of $24 each way. Trouble is, this only covers a fraction of the $5.25 million cost of providing the service over the next year so state taxpayers will provide a subsidy for about 90 percent of the ride. Federal taxpayers will also chip in smaller amounts for start-up costs and other incidentals. In order for this service to pay for itself, ridership on the route would have to be 600 passengers per day, almost ten times higher than what Amtrak projects. But even this is impossible, since the train assigned to make the run can carry only 288 passengers.

Although federal freight railroads have been successfully privatized, taxpayers are still hauling Amtrak's fat caboose. Rep. Ernest Istook (R-OK) discovered that Oklahoma City Limousine services would provide door-to-door service to Ft Worth and back along with chauffeuring while in Texas for an average of $450—less than the full-subsidized cost of a single round trip train ride.

Capital Ideas
July/August 1999

CHAPTER 5

The next day brought a hard steady rain and upon entering the Commons area, Hugh couldn't help but wonder if the even larger crowd was there to hear about Russia under communism or to just escape the elements.

"Dobri utra," he greeted the assemblage. "As long as you're learning about Russian history, you might as well pick up a little of their language. I just greeted you with 'Good Morning.' Now has anyone been able to bone up on any of the problems I left with you?"

One lady—young lady?—she looked as though she was barely past puberty—raised her hand and said,

"Sir, I am too young to have witnessed everything that has transpired in education but as I plan to study to become a teacher someday, I have made a rather thorough study of education problems. If you would be so kind as to tell me the problems that existed in that field before you lost contact with our world, perhaps that would give me a starting point."

"Alright," Hugh replied. "I'll start back at the snow scene so you can get the drift. I probably should point out that I used to do stand-up comedy as a hobby, so if my humor seems to be what we used to call 'corny,' please bear with me.

"The last things I recall about the problems that existed in the educational field in 2000 were such items as the vast amounts of money that was being thrown at our schools and the lack of learning that we were getting for our tax dollars. People were concerned about the lack of discipline coupled with criminal violence. We were told that many high school graduates couldn't even read their own diplomas. The schools were giving what was jokingly referred to as 'social promotions' just to get the kids out of their classes. When I went back to the city where I was born, Council Bluffs, Iowa, I visited my alma mater and couldn't believe they offered classes in remedial reading in high school. In my day, if we couldn't read, we flunked, pure and simple.

"Upon checking with Clark College in Vancouver, Washington, I was shocked to learn the high percentage of high school graduates that were required to take courses in 'bone-head' English and 'bone-head' math. Of course, one has to factor in the fact that Clark is a Community College, and, as such, does not require a high school diploma to matriculate. Also many students at such institutions are mature adults who haven't cracked a book in years.

"Perhaps one can get a better picture from a regular four year institution such as Washington State University. A check with them revealed that in the September 2000 class year, of about 3,000 freshmen, 607 were required to take remedial math. We were told that many schools no longer taught geography, and history had become an elective. Indeed, it seemed that many young people didn't know which countries bordered the United States on the north and south nor could they find America on a globe of the world. I had occasion to give talks at various high schools in the Vancouver, Washington area and couldn't help but notice the teachers never bothered to correct student grammar.

"Speaking of grammar, or the lack thereof, I even had correspondence with Dr. Lois DeBakey, a professor who divided her time between Baylor and Tulane. At that time she was conducting a one-woman war with Nashville for what Music City was doing to our language. It was like peeing in the Pacific to raise the tide, but, bless her heart, she certainly gave it her best shot. I hadn't corresponded with her for quite some time but often wondered how she must have felt about rock and roll and I bet she really lost it when a new racket appeared on the scene called Rap, another noise that a candy striper introduced me to last week.

"There were pros and cons about school vouchers and some folks were absolutely paranoid, for they were afraid some private school would be getting tax money. They lost sight of the objective, which was to educate the populace. It took only one Protestant to scream that a Catholic might get two cents of his tax money to throw a monkey wrench into the voucher concept in many areas. Of course, the age-old argument of separation of church and state kept rearing its ugly head. One of the biggest flies in the ointment was the NEA—National Education Association—as they fought vouchers tooth and toenail. They were already feeling the effects of 'home schooling' and some wondered just how insecure their perch might have become. Don't get me wrong, they still wielded a big club for they were able to get up to thirty-three percent of the delegates to the Democrat National Conventions.

"I was able to personally witness the decline in the American educational system. When I was a kid—(yes, I had to walk five miles each way to and from school through six foot snow drifts at twenty below zero and it was uphill each way). My school had no cafeteria or gymnasium. We were taught the three Rs—later amended to four when they added Ritalin. We learned geography in the fourth grade and had to memorize the name of every state in the union and its capital. As I recall, we learned short division also at that level. In the fifth, we were exposed to history, long division and fractions. The sixth grade offered us decimals and the seventh presented us with some very difficult thought problems.

"Back in the thirties and forties, students from rural schools in Pottawattamie County, Iowa, who wished to attend one of the Council Bluffs high schools were subjected to an entrance exam, a test that most high school graduates in the year 2000 would have been hard pressed to pass. The test was administered by the County, up until the time the rural school districts were consolidated in the late forties. If times have changed that much in a relatively short span what must have transpired while I've been away?"

The very young lady volunteer, who identified herself as Harriette Angel, came to the front of the group and thanked Mr. Williams for his outline on the subject and as to what was occurring way back in the year 2000.

"Now that you have been so kind as to give me a starting point, I'll attempt to fill in the missing pieces to the educational puzzle. I do not claim to be an expert on the subject, so if anyone in the audience can correct me or add anything, I would be more than pleased to relinquish time for them to elucidate.

"Mr. Williams, you mentioned vouchers and, indeed, they have become as common today as food stamps were in your day. Try as they might, the teachers' unions couldn't escape the fact that private and home schools were turning out a better product than most public schools. Oh, we still hear the same ol', same ol' church-and-state arguments, but when a few folks, who put education first, dug up the examples of the success of the G.I. Bill of Rights utilized after World War II, those bureaucrats had most of the wind taken from their sails. It was pointed out that the men and women, returning from the service, who chose private schools, were not tarnished by the education they received at such institutions as Notre Dame and Stanford.

"After all, the G.I. Bill was nothing but a voucher system and it worked extremely well. Now, in the year 2020, the unions are still around, but now they must adhere to a system of quality education instead of electing delegates to national conventions to vote for abortion. Now schools must compete on the open market and as the cream rises to the top, the failures became history. In fact, many of the union members actually coerced their fellow staff members to deliver a quality product to protect all their jobs.

"One major change that took place in many unions, as far as that goes, was a restriction against forcing members to contribute to candidates and causes they did not believe in. With their teeth pulled when it came to lobbying, they were forced to pursue other endeavors, which in the long run, improved the quality of their unions and the whole teaching profession. Back around the turn of the century, some states, such as Massachusetts, decided it was time to reward good teachers and persuade the bad ones to seek another line of work. Indeed, they even paid signing bonuses as high as $20,000.

"As for prayers in school, that argument is still being bandied about, however between a combination of defiance and School Board members looking the other way, student-led prayers are being conducted nationwide. It probably got its start in small cities in the Midwest where annually students held a prayer meeting on the school grounds. It grew in popularity until school officials decided they couldn't put the toothpaste back in the tube and, reluctantly at first, acquiesced. There was still an element that insisted that no mention of God, Jesus or the Bible be allowed at graduation exercises so one class decided to sing all stanzas of the 'Star Spangled Banner.' An atheist complained but when the School Board considered how the headlines would read, they turned a deaf ear to the complaint. They just couldn't bear the publicity such as 'Entire Senior Class Arrested for Singing Our National Anthem.'

"Needless to say, the idea spread like wildfire and the practice was copied immediately, especially in the Bible belt. Even the United States Supreme Court looked the other way but strongly recommended that any other religion in a given school student body be given equal treatment if so requested. The fact that parents of America got up on their high horse and demanded more local control contributed largely to the new freedom of religion and even curricula.

"It took many years to do so, but a majority finally realized that federal funds with federal controls were likened to giving oneself a transfusion from their right arm to their left arm and spilling half the blood in the process. I understand that back in the year 2000, billions of dollars were owed to the federal government in unpaid student loans. Not so, today. They finally cracked down and with computer tracing, as soon as one's social security number shows up on a job application, bells ring, lights flash and Uncle Sugar is there for his payments. This method, I might add, has been used extensively in the case of dead-beat parents who have defaulted on child support.

"Back in about 2010, the consensus finally concluded that for some youngsters, school, as it had been structured for years, was just not for every one. Let's face it, everybody is not college material so it was decided, in many districts, that upon completion of the tenth grade, students would be at the crossroads of their schooling and were allowed to remain in traditional high school curricula and prepare for college or they could opt to take up a trade. Teachers welcomed this innovation, as it tended to weed many disruptive students from their classes. After all, why teach Shakespeare to a young dude that wants to be an airline mechanic? Some cities, such as Phoenix had experienced much success with such a program.

"I think it is safe to say the reason for the big decline in the drop-out rate was the new laws, enacted by many states, to the effect that a youth had to prove he was enrolled in a recognized institution of learning, have a diploma from same or have reached his eighteenth birthday or no driver's license.

"With the advent of vouchers, it was no longer practical to furnish transportation for students. Hadn't some folks questioned for years that it did not make sense to spend five million dollars for a gymnasium for exercise and another five million dollars for buses so the kids didn't have to walk? Of course, in more affluent areas, if the parents wanted wheels for their youngsters and were willing to pay for it, so be it. The new expanded local control of the schools, coupled with myriad Charter Schools, permit such freedoms.

"Many high schools have opted for ROTC—Reserve Officer Training Corps—programs and while the pacifists complained bitterly many folks actually believe the discipline it offers has reduced juvenile delinquency. Of course having a uniform to wear to school three days a week greatly reduced additional strain on the clothing budget. The students are able to attend two weeks summer intensive training at a military installation. Of course, this is co-educational as is the rest of the program and is strictly voluntary. Speaking of the military, wasn't it about the time of your accident that the Public Schools in Portland, Oregon decided not to let armed forces recruiters on their campuses? Well, the withholding of federal funds changed their tune. Indeed, it was one of the few incidents where the federal money, or the withholding thereof, actually accomplished a desired goal of a majority.

"I've been told that back around the turn of the century, you had a system of corrections in school that provided a private tutor for students that had been expelled. This made absolutely no sense and we understand that some students preferred this treatment and had little problem in achieving this status. Not so today. If a student is expelled, he risks flunking the grade, depending on the length of expulsion. If he is a repeater, as it had already been proved that jail did more harm than good, the name was conveniently made available to the powers that be in the State Drivers License department and the eighteen-year-old clause was removed from his eligibility. It took only a few bad apples to bring the point home, so this problem now is almost non-existent.

"Oh yes, geography is now being taught in nearly every school in the nation. The liberals are still asking about the need for it in this highly technological age, but we merely point out it was they that kept preaching to us about the global economy. Would you believe there are some, although they discarded such labels as socialists and communists, who still carry the torch for one-world government?

"Perhaps the biggest single issue came to the forefront when a syndicated columnist wrote a rather extensive article on the state of many of America's public schools. He had the audacity to actually publish a spelling test such as the following—try these on your seven-year old:

humanity, execution, industrious, satisfaction, beautiful, multitudes, immediately, dominion, brethren, affliction, amusement, amounting, obedient, remained, particular, permission, wanton, grieved, remember, cruelty, cultivated, believed, plaintive, patience, frightened, promised, murdered, Philadelphia, increase, ignorant, hardships, disgraced, destruction, property, Pennsylvania, disrespectful, usefulness, providentially, unfortunately.

"If your child is unable to spell most of these words, know their meaning and use them in a sentence, I strongly recommend that you, as an interested parent, along with members of the PTA, march right down to your local school board and demand that your education taxes return more bang for your buck. You may want to take a lesson from the protesters of years gone by and be sure you are accompanied by media reporters. Oh, incidentally, you might take this list with you and explain that these are just a few of the words second-graders learned back in 1836. Yes, these are right out of *McGuffy's Eclectic Second Reader*. If that doesn't make you feel like a penny waiting for change, how do these first-grade words grab ya?" Deranged, frightfully, elegant, poisoned, instructed, commandment, penitence, miserable, etc. ad infinitum.

"Saving the best example till last, try this test on high-school graduates—it was taken from the original document on file at the Smokey Valley Genealogical Society and Library in Salina, Kansas and was reprinted by the *Salina Journal*:

8th Grade Final Exam: Salina, KS—1895

Grammar (Time: one hour)

1. Give nine rules for the use of Capital Letters.

2. Name the Parts of Speech and define those that have no modifications.

3. Define Verse, Stanza and Paragraph.

4. What are the Principal Parts of a Verb? Give Principal Parts of do, lie, lay and run.

5. Define Case. Illustrate each Case.

6. What is Punctuation? Give rules for principal marks of Punctuation.

7-10. Write a composition of about 150 words and show therein that you understand the practical use of the rules of grammar.

Arithmetic (Time: 1.25 hours)

1. Name and define the Fundamental Rules of Arithmetic.

2. A wagon box is 2-ft. deep, 10-feet long and 3-ft. wide. How many bushels of wheat will it hold?

3. If a load of wheat weighs 3,942 lbs., what is it worth at 50 cents per bu., deducting 1,050 lbs. for tare?

4. District No. 33 has a valuation of $35,000. What is the necessary levy to carry on a school seven months at $50 per month, and have $104 for incidentals?

5. Find cost of 6,720 lbs. of coal at $6.00 per ton.

6. Find the interest on $512.60 for 8 months and 18 days at 7 percent.

7. What is the cost of 40 boards 12-inches wide and 16-ft. long at $20 per M?

8. Find bank discount on $300 for 90 days (no grace) at 10 percent.

9. What is the cost of a square farm at $15 per acre, the distance around which is 640 rods?

10. Write a Bank Check, a Promissory Note and a Receipt.

U.S. History (Time: 45 minutes)

1. Give the epochs into which U.S. History is divided.

2. Give an account of the discovery of America by Columbus.

3. Relate the causes and results of the Revolutionary War.

4. Show the territorial growth of the United States.

5. Tell what you can of the history of Kansas.

6. Describe three of the most prominent battles of the Rebellion.

7. Who were the following: Morse, Whitney, Fulton, Bell, Lincoln, Penn and Howe?

8. Name events connected with the following dates: 1607 1620 1800 1849 1865

Orthography (Time: one hour)

1. What is meant by the following: Alphabet, phonetic, orthography, etymology, syllabication?

2. What are elementary sounds? How classified?

3. What are the following and give examples of each: Trigraph, subvocals, diphthong, cognate letters, linguals?

4. Give four substitutes for caret 'u.'

5. Give two rules for spelling words with final 'e.' Name two exceptions of each rule.

6. Give two uses of silent letters in spelling. Illustrate each.

7. Define the following prefixes and use in connection with a word: Bi, dis, mis, pre, semi, post, non, inter, mono, super.

8. Mark diacritically and divide into syllables the following and name the sign that indicates the sound: Card, ball, mercy, sir, odd, cell, rise, blood, fare, last.

9. Use the following correctly in sentences:

Cite,	site,	sight,
fane,	fain,	feign,
vane,	vain,	vein,
raze,	raise,	rays.

10. Write 10 words frequently mispronounced and indicate pronunciation by use of diacritical marks and by syllabication.

Geography (Time: one hour)

1. What is climate? Upon what does climate depend?

2. How do you account for the extremes of climate in Kansas?

3. Of what use are rivers? Of what use is the ocean?

4. Describe the mountains of North America.

5. Name and describe the following: Monrovia, Odessa, Denver, Manitoba, Hecla, Yukon, St. Helena, Juan Fermandez, Aspinwall and Orinoco.

1. Name and locate the principal trade centers of the U.S.

2. Name all the Republics of Europe and give capital of each.

3. Why is the Atlantic Coast colder than the Pacific in the same latitude?

4. Describe the process by which the water of the ocean returns to the source of rivers.

5. Describe the movements of the earth. Give inclination of the earth.

Physiology (Time: 45 minutes)

1. Where are the saliva, gastric juice and bile secreted? What is the use of each in digestion?

2. How does nutrition reach the circulation?

3. What is the function of the liver? Of the kidneys?

4. How would you stop the flow of blood from an artery in case of laceration?

5. Give some general directions that you think would be beneficial to preserve the human body in good health.

"Imagine a college student trying to pass this test, even if the few outdated questions were modernized. Gives the saying of an early-twentieth-century person that 'she/he had only an eighth grade education' a whole new meaning.

"Federal funds for education also had a flip side. All that money was just too enticing for some school districts to walk away from. Indeed, one teacher in a middle school in Southwest Washington complained that the school, if not the district, was deliberately dumbing down the students that resulted in lower SAT scores, hence more of that 'free' money from Uncle Sam. The area had a disproportionate number of immigrants, some legal along with many so-called refugees and most of the youngsters from those groups were placed in ESL (English as a Second Language) classes. When some of the parents complained and insisted their children be mainstreamed, their test scores rose dramatically and most were speaking English in as little as three months. Similar reports came from California, which had discontinued teaching in foreign languages about that time. Incidentally that teacher was fired.

"Well, Mr. Williams, have I worn out my welcome?"

"You'll have to ask the audience," Hugh replied, "but from the looks of the audience, I'd say you held their interest almost as much as you held mine. In fact, I think they should be given college credit for the course. While we're on the subject of education, I'd like to add the story of an incident that occurred to me back in about 2000.

"I remember suggesting to my Rotary Club that we have some small copies of the Constitution and The Declaration of Independence printed and distributed in school. My experience with handouts by the American Legion and the 40 et 8—Honor Society of the Legion—showed that while the first-grade kids enjoyed the American flags we gave them, the novelty wore off in a couple of days. To me, it demonstrated symbolism without substance. Our club had adopted the Hazel Dell Grade School and it was decided these documents would be handed out to the fifth-grade students. By adoption, I refer to the fact our club participated in a 'lunch buddy' program with that grade school that provided for our members to accompany a student to lunch at least once a month. These youngsters came from primarily one-parent families and the mentoring was priceless.

"During the process of handing out the little books containing the

Constitution, a few of our Rotary club members gave a little talk. I told the students about America's wars from the Revolution through the Cold War. I told them that after eight trips to Russia and seeing the results of that country's seventy-five-year 'experiment with socialism,' as they called it, I could come to but one conclusion; the only good communist was a dead one. Evidently I struck a nerve as in the fall I was informed I was persona non-grata at that grade school and being a bad influence, I could not have a lunch buddy. I hope none of those students viewed *The History Channel* as the night before I made my presentation; I saw the history of the Solidarity movement in Poland with the members carrying huge banners proclaiming that same sentiment."

"You'll be happy to learn, Hugh," responded Harriette. "that many changes have taken place in our schools while you were sleeping. Don't know if your little tiff with the Vancouver School District struck a nerve or it was the dastardly attack by terrorists on 9/11, but certain films are now required viewing in the schools. Finally realizing that man would be just as enslaved by the extreme right-wing as they would be under the extreme left-wing, today's kids are exposed to such films as '*Hitler's Children*' and '*Stalin, Man of Steel*.'"

"Now, how many would like another session tomorrow?" Hugh asked. If there was anyone missing from among the outstretched arms Hugh Williams was unable to observe them. "Okay, same, time, same place. See ya' all tomorrow."

FLOODGATE

Reporters found the pun too wet to resist but taxpayers and consumers may be the ones who got soaked the hardest by "Floodgate", the latest fiscal scandal surrounding Vice President Al Gore.

On July 22, 1999, Pacific Gas and Electric opened the floodgates of its dam in New Hampshire to raise the level of the Connecticut River about ten inches—all to make sure that Al Gore's canoe didn't get mired in the mud at a photo opportunity at which he touted—what else?—A $100,000 federal grant to the river's Joint Commission. Reactions to this order by the Secret Service and the Joint Commission were swifter than Whitewater rapids. Vermont's Natural Resources Director told reporters, "they won't release water for the fish when we ask them to, but somehow they find themselves able to release it for politicians." The Veep's spinsters tried to sell the press down the river but the truth beat them there: half a billion gallons were released, the gates were kept open twice as long as usual, it required employee overtime and rerouted power grids, and the value of the wasted water to residents was close to $1 million. Gore's environmentalist tome 'Earth in the Balance" warned that 'increased per capita (water) use' could lead to 'revolutionary political disorder.'

Capital Ideas
September/October 1999

CHAPTER 6

Over the clinking of coffee cups and idle chatter, Hugh Williams, or 'professor' as some of his protégé 's started to refer to him, started to bring the 'class' to order. "Okay", one participant announced, "now the ball is in *your* court. If these sessions are tit for tat, it's now your turn to fill us in on what happened upon your arrival in Leningrad nearly fifty years ago."

"Alright folks, if you're sure you really want to hear it and are not just being kind to an old man, I'll continue, but on the condition that those of you who fall asleep will refrain from snoring. I may be getting up in years, but, as you can see, I haven't lost my sense of humor.

"Before we had left my hometown of Vancouver, Washington, Winnie had told everyone that she was going to take a roll of adhesive tape to cover my mouth in Russia. She was sure that, feeling the way I did about communism, I would surely end up in the salt mines. Long before we departed the Leningrad airport, however, I heard her mutter, 'these expletive, expletive communists.' Who would have believed that I would be the one to remind *her* to cool it?

"After loading our luggage into the car, we set out for the city. I was surprised that it was such a great distance from the airport. Perhaps the biggest difference in the scenery from the West was the complete lack of advertising and the drabness of the buildings. Driving into town, one could not help but notice what were obviously green belts between huge apartment complexes. We were very surprised to see so many people on the streets shopping at the rather late hour of eight in the evening. The streets were actu-

Soviet soft drink and water vending machines

ally crowded with hundreds of soldiers, sailors and their girlfriends, many of whom were eating ice cream. On the sidewalks there were rows of soft-drink vending machines dispensing their national beverage known as *kvas* and water.

Everyone drank from the same glass, which they claimed was sterilized between servings. We were later informed by a tour guide that this was their 'Coca Cola' and was made from yeast, syrup, sugar and water.

"We finally arrived at the Leningrad Hotel and were impressed by such a modern building. But, like a book, Russia could not be judged by the facade it presented at first glance. While the hotel was only two years old, it seemed that out of seven elevators, only two were functioning. This must have been anticipated for comfortable furniture was provided in front of the elevators on every floor for what could be up to a fifteen-minute wait. After finally getting checked in, which involved the surrender of our passports, we were in the mood for a tall cool one. We proceeded to the dining room on the main floor only to be informed that it was reserved for tour groups only.

"I decided to go back to the rather hefty blonde that had checked us in and obtain more information about the hotel's facilities. When I told her I wanted some information she replied '*nyet*.' I said '*da*,' and her answer was 'no information, information tomorrow morning at nine thirty'. By this time, I was beginning to lose my patience and I think it showed for she then volunteered…'bar, ninth floor'.

"After what seemed like a long dry wait, we were finally able to secure an elevator going up. Stepping out on the ninth floor, we couldn't believe our eyes and ears. A beautiful bar, complete with stereo, greeted us. It turned out to be what was commonly referred to as a 'dollar' bar or one of the places where they accepted western currency only. After a couple of screwdrivers, I asked the Russian bartender if he had anything on the stereo besides Russian folk music? He said 'what do you want? Johnny Cash?' When I answered in the affirmative, he promptly put on a Johnny Cash album followed by Tom Jones. Indeed, it was difficult to imagine we were in the Soviet Union.

"Later, we went up to the tenth floor, for we had been told we could be served some dinner there. We ordered beef potted thinking we would be served pot roast. It turned out to be more like a stew with lots of vegetables and meat. It really wasn't too bad until we bit into what we thought was a large piece of meat only to discover it was liver. The cost of the dinners, including some beer and wine, was less than seven dollars total and they accepted American currency.

"From the tenth floor dining room, we had a panoramic view of the city. We could look across the Neva River and see that the skyline was dotted with domes and spires. Directly across an estuary from the hotel, at anchor, was the cruiser *Aurora*.

It was from this vessel that the first shot was fired that signaled the start of the 1917 Revolution. The next morning, we slept in but the longing for a cup of coffee got me up before Winnie was awake. I

Cruiser Aurora

went down to the main dining room to be informed that if I wanted only coffee, I would have to go to a buffet, one of which was located on each even numbered floor. I had tasted bad coffee in Western Europe, but this was impossible. It required a lot of milk and sugar to disguise the taste.

"I went back to the room to find Winnie ready and waiting for me to take her to breakfast. Having already been informed that we must eat on the tenth floor, I pressed the button for the elevator then sat down for the usual wait. In the restaurant, we were seated immediately but were offered no menus. In the Soviet Union, all hotel rooms were rented including at least breakfast and one took what was served. The waiter brought eggs in the individual pans they had been fried in along with black bread and marmalade. We had this same breakfast every day we were in the Soviet Union, however, sometimes they included what they called sausage but we would call salami back home.

"The pans were sizzling hot with the result the eggs were burned on the bottom but raw on the top. If we quickly stirred them, we ended up with a form of scrambled eggs that was just tolerable. When we were able to make ourselves understood, we asked for the eggs to be turned over and we ended up with omelets. I shall never forget that first breakfast when they served what we thought was milk. I took one sip and nearly gagged. It tasted like buttermilk and I noticed the other guests left their glasses untouched. Every menu included what they called fermented milk, but we would call it yogurt. I tried what they called fresh milk but could not drink it so we did not have a glass of milk all the time we were in Russia.

"After that first breakfast, we went down to the Intourist Service Bureau only to be informed we could not exchange our vouchers for coupons until afternoon. Having time to kill, we decided to take a boat ride as we had observed many sightseeing boats on the river and estuaries. Seeking a taxi we were offered the service of an Intourist driver. We asked him to take us to the boat landing across the river and he seemed to understand. Upon arrival at the boat dock, he insisted on taking us to another boat landing a half a mile down the river. He thought he was doing us a favor by taking us to the hydra-foil landing and we couldn't make him understand that we had already ridden such a craft between Copenhagen and Malmo, Sweden and merely wanted a leisurely picture-taking trip at a little slower pace.

"The ride with this man was a hair-raising experience, as he seemed to be musically inclined and with his radio turned up full blast, he nodded his head in time with the music while pretending to conduct a symphony orchestra. As I recall, the song on his car radio was '*Raindrops Keep Falling on My Head.*' I often wondered if the Russians translated that song literally as it did contain the message: 'because I'm free.' It was a case of ' 'look, Ma, no hands' as we traveled at break-neck speed through the city. The so-called wild drivers of Paris and Tokyo couldn't hold a candle to the Russians. When they got behind the wheel, they were like kids with new toys, which, in fact, they were.

"We boarded the boat after purchasing tickets to an unknown destination. Immediately we headed for the aft end of the craft, which was open, permitting better shots with our cameras. The vessel was a real antique and we wondered about its worthiness. We proceeded across the Neva River right by our hotel offering us an excellent photo opportunity of both the Leningrad Hotel and the cruiser *Aurora*. Shortly after departure, a Russian offered me one of his cigarettes. As I didn't want to start an international incident, I politely accepted. The filter was twice as long as the tobacco portion. Upon lighting it, my fear of communism was reduced by about fifty percent for if the average Russian smoked those things, they would surely perish.

"During the upstream trip, I thought I overheard a word or two of English. When I worked my way over to the other side of the boat to the source of that conversation they reverted to Russian. It was a young fellow with his girlfriend on a Sunday holiday and probably practicing what they had learned in school. I tried to communicate with him using my best Pidgin English. They both at least pretended not to understand but I was persistent. When we reached the end of the line, at what turned out to be an amusement park, I tried to ask him if we were to purchase tickets for the return trip. He motioned for us to remain on board but returned shortly and pointed to a ticket office on shore. We walked up to the ticket office and purchased two return tickets, which cost less than twenty-five cents each. As we were returning to the boat, the Russian couple was walking up to the park. I yelled '*Spaseba*' which meant thank you and, much to my surprise and disgust, he replied, 'Don't mention it'. He had a grin a mile wide and seemed to take great delight in his joke.

"If you're not completely turned off by now, you never will be," Williams commented, "but if you want more, I'm game if you are. However, suppose we skip a day so none of us gets burned out. That will give me some much needed rest and provide you with a little more time for researching the questions I have asked of you."

NAVY GRAVY

How many reports of $500 toilet seats will it take for the federal gov-
ernment to stamp out contractor fraud? Well, they're still counting.
Thanks to an FBI-led operation, criminal charges have been filed
against 21 individuals with firms that had maintenance contracts
with the U.S. Navy. This one investigation focused solely upon $200
million in repair deals made between 1995 and 1999, on eight sea-lift
vessels. Although the government made sure that the repairs were
actually completed, it took 27 agents to follow the money into the
pockets of the alleged rip-off artists. And deep those pockets were: the
FBI alleges that the accused diverted taxpayer dollars from their contracts for golf outings, trips to the Belmont Stakes horse race, boats,
grand pianos, televisions, private school tuition and even payments
to a girlfriend. Because the FBI's audit is ongoing, the total loss to
taxpayers is unknown but almost certain to climb into seven figures.
Taxpayers should applaud the FBI's work but it took four years and
dozens of agents to flush the fat out of a tiny fraction of the Defense
Department's $275 billion budget.

Capital Ideas
September/October 1999

CHAPTER 7

The day off passed like a jet plane and Hugh's mind was humming like a well-oiled machine. He hoped the members of his class were having the same experience. If there was any loss of interest, it certainly wasn't manifested by the attendance after the one-day bye.

The next day's session was scheduled for late afternoon to accommodate a large group of students that had expressed their desire to attend one of the now well-known living history lessons. The sun was starting to cast long shadows but neither Hugh nor his audience needed that to tell them that their buns were not cast of steel.

"*Dobri den* to my political advisors" was the greeting the "students" were met with after their one day off. "I hope none of you did anything I would liked to have done yesterday."

While most of his audience responded with polite laughter, nobody had the heart to call his jokes "like from nowhere, man." When it came to humor, there was nearly as much of a generation gap as there always seemed to be in what some folks call music. If their future sessions with the "professor" were anything like the previous ones, they could bear to humor him and what he thought was comedy in exchange for what they came to feel was "living history."

"Well, according to my presidulator, I believe it's your serve," announced Mr. Williams as he opened the discussion.

"Who is prepared to surprise me today and with what subject?" With that a young fellow that appeared to be only about eighteen was the first to volunteer.

"Sir, I don't claim to be an expert on any subject, but you have sparked my interest in a field that, until last week, I couldn't have cared less about. Would you believe I have asked many older folks about their recollection of the last twenty years and I even spent some time yesterday in the library?"

"I'm glad to hear you admit you're not an expert," responded Hugh, "for in my day, an expert was described as follows: an ex is a has-been and a spurt is a drip under pressure." Finally the "Professor" came up with a joke that, while corny, was so old many of the 'students' hadn't heard it.

"Son, just what subject are you going to bring us up to speed on today?"

"Please sir, just call me Jason and with your permission, I'd like to pass along what I found has happened during the last twenty years in the field of Constitutional rights...Keep in mind I am too young to remember many of the incidents I am passing along so I had to depend on other sources.

"Yesterday, I took the time to read the U.S. Constitution and was amazed at what I saw. Now I know why we have passed some of the laws that I kept reading about but never understood. I only wish now I had paid more attention in those government classes that I was forced to attend.

"While I didn't have time to do the research I would liked to have done, perhaps I can shed some light on the positions taken in regard to the First, Second, Fifth and Tenth Amendments. This whole bit about the Constitution and the Declaration of Independence has caused me to change my major when I matriculate at the university this fall. I'm now opting for Poli-Sci.

"As I see it, the First Amendment guarantees us the freedom of speech. However, I found that in your day, some folks had more freedom than others. I've heard that in some colleges and universities, a professor would be allowed to utter anything that suited his fancy. However, in one case where an instructor made a derogatory remark about former President Reagan and a student that didn't share his views, disagreed publicly, that student would have been given an F or even kicked out of school. Such action is not tolerated today. With so many students 'wearing a wire', not to nail professors, but for reviewing lectures, it would be foolish for faculty members to stifle challenges.

"As you know, many, many years ago, a distinguished Supreme Court Justice ruled that freedom of speech did not permit one to shout 'fire' in a crowded theater and I'm sure nobody disputes that. However, in our day we now believe that some individuals and institutions have carried our First Amendment freedoms too far. At some time, we, as a nation, lost track of the difference between freedom and license. You are free to swing a fist at me but the minute that fist contacts my nose, that freedom becomes license. In other words, you are free to say almost anything as long as it doesn't hurt anyone else. That's what prompted slander laws.

"Looking back, many of us nowadays wonder just what was going though folks' minds when they declared that nude dancing was a form of expression and therefore protected under freedom of speech. Why did the taxpayers of your day permit their money to be spent funding porno in our libraries? Yes, I read that many liberal newspapers screamed censorship when some folks tried to remove that filth, but it was years before the courts wised up to the fact that as long as this material was available in smut stores, censorship, as such, didn't exist.

"Speaking of smut, the NEA—National Endowment for the Arts— was one of the biggest culprits. Why did your generation allow characters like Mapplethorpe to urinate in a bottle, insert a crucifix, label it *Piss Christ,* pawn it off as art and get paid with taxpayer's funds? There were other examples of funded porn, but there are some youngsters in our audience and even trying to describe some of that subsidized filth is not fit for young ears.

"There have been volumes written about all the amendments but it does appear that early in this century, wiser heads finally prevailed and we now accept the Constitution as it was written and intended by the Founding Fathers and not by the interpretation of some old folks in long robes that try to inject their personal liberal feelings into our laws. As in your day, Professor, there were way-out groups that insisted they were being denied their constitutional rights when courts mandated that some of their off-the-wall, odd-ball rituals didn't come under that category.

"As for the Second Amendment, not much has changed in that area. Folks are still battling it out regarding guns, but fortunately the pro-gun forces are rapidly gaining favor as they have history on their side. It seems to me, Mr. Williams that Australia experimented with an attempt to disarm the citizenry around the turn of the century and the anti-gun people nearly croaked when statistics revealed that the crime rate in that country rose dramatically. As this was way before my time, I can only speculate that because many folks in those days could remember Hitler, Mussolini, Stalin and Tojo they could keep reminding succeeding generations that those vicious murderous dictators were able to rise to power because the populace was unarmed. While I'm sure the average American, in those days, didn't think that the federal government would use force against its own citizens, there had been just enough incidents of overkill to keep our citizenry on its feet.

"Now many cities have offered their police department training facilities, especially their target ranges, for use by ordinary citizens.

Ladies flocked to the pistol ranges when it became generally known that so many people, who thought owning a gun would protect them, actually had their own weapons used against them. Not so, nowadays. Woe onto the thug that attacks a lady who has spent some time at one of the gun handling facilities. That, coupled with the fact that virtually every women in America carries mace, has reduced crimes against women by the thousands. Car-jacking, as you knew it in your day, is virtually non-existent today.

"On the flip side of the coin, even the NRA—National Rifle Association—in addition to educating the populace on the proper care and use of a weapon actually lobbied vehemently for stricter laws governing the use of a gun in connection with any type of crime. They were successful in getting legislation passed in most states to the effect that the sentence for any crime in which a firearm is used will automatically add ten years to the incarceration. Crime, as you probably remember it before your accident, is but a fraction of what it was, partly due to the sensible gun laws, but also due to other legislation. I would elaborate on that subject, but I might be stealing someone else's thunder.

"What has happened in regard to the Fifth Amendment while you were 'away?' I don't know about your day, but I read that some governmental jurisdictions were abusing the so-called Right of Eminent Domain. In many areas there grew to be what some folks referred to as little 'fiefdoms' complete with little Hitlers. In some counties, land would be seized and not only were the landowners not compensated, they were forced to pay for roads nobody wanted. This was known as 'takings' and it took many, many lawsuits before government wised up and that practice is virtually unheard of today."

At this point, Hugh Williams interrupted with an apology and remarked:

"I happen to have first-hand knowledge in that field so let me add to your wonderful research. Back before the turn of the century, there was a firm in Tigard, Oregon that applied to the city fathers for a building permit to construct an addition to their plumbing and electrical supply warehouse. They were told that in order to obtain such a permit, they would have to 'dedicate', another term for donate, a chunk of land to the city for a bicycle path. When the applicant refused and quoted the Fifth Amendment, the city fathers laughed. The hardware firm had offered to sell the land to the city for $14,000 but was ignored. After exhausting all legal avenues, the case finally went to the United States Supreme Court and they ruled in favor of the plaintiff, citing the Fifth Amendment. When another application for the building permit was denied, the hardware people sued the City of Tigard for $2 million. The City settled for $1.5 million thus paying an astronomical sum for what could have been obtained for $14,000.

"In my own Clark County the practice of 'takings' had been prevalent for many years. A small developer by the name of Burt Lance had purchased a small piece of land after having been assured he could short plat it into three or four lots. The county then changed its mind and informed Mr. Lance that he would 'dedicate' a strip of land through the plat and pay for a street, complete with curbs and sidewalks. Keep in mind, the neighbors did not want the street and it served no purpose, as it would dead-end at the next property. The owner of that piece did not want to sell her land. She should have known that as soon as the county confiscated Mr. Lance's property they would give her the same treatment when she decided to subdivide.

"After a couple of years or so, Burt met with the county and offered to sell them the strip they desired for $15,000 but the county laughed and said, 'no, we are going to get it and it won't cost us a cent.' That was easy for them to say as they were fighting the citizens with the citizens' own money. Talk about deep pockets, the county attorney has unlimited funds so the average developer, knowing 'you can't fight city hall,' just rolls over and plays dead. That's what Mr. Lance probably should have done, but he decided to dig in and fight for his constitutional rights. The county literally put Mr. Lance out of business for as long as any litigation was hanging over his head; his line of credit was pulled at any and all lending institutions.

"The case was heard twice in local courts and each time, the judge ruled in Burt's favor but the county still didn't give up and took it to Superior Court in Tacoma. Again the verdict was that it was a 'takings' pure and simple but by this time, Burt's legal fees were astronomical. Finally the county reluctantly purchased the land for something over $190,000 but it was too late for Burt. That sum didn't make a dent in the debts he had incurred and he kept meticulous records on the opportunities he had to forego because of what his government had done to him. Again, here was a case of the government using our tax money to fight us and blowing over a hundred and ninety grand, for a parcel they could have purchased earlier for fifteen thousand.

"I had first hand knowledge of this case as I accompanied Burt Lance to a luncheon meeting with a lady—Busse Nutley—who was a County Commissioner at that time. I asked her why she insisted on trampling on her constituent's constitutional rights and her reply was 'because we have always done it that way and we always will.' I understand the county has passed new laws addressing these problems but it's a little late for Burt Lance. I always wondered why the home building industry and real estate interests never came to his aid.

"Sorry, I interrupted, but you touched on a subject that was dear to me and I can't help but wonder what is taking place today in regard to property rights."

"Well," replied the young 'student,' "perhaps your friend did the whole nation a favor, as such cases nowadays are unheard of. I do believe the subsequent publicity created a new awareness in the people and now perhaps as many copies of our Constitution are found in our homes as Bibles. The value of our rights is now being emphasized in school and most youngsters can recite the first Ten Amendments verbatim….

"While all of the Amendments are vital to our free society, time did not permit me to delve into all of them so my contribution to our 'school' will conclude with a discussion of the Tenth. Mr. Williams, you may recall that back before the turn of the century, there was a move afoot to get various states to pass what became known as the Tenth Amendment Resolution. I believe that Colorado and perhaps other states passed such a resolution but it took what seemed forever to educate folks as to just what the Tenth Amendment is. I'm sure you know it reads as follows: 'The powers not delegated to the United States by the Constitution, nor prohibited by it to the States, are pre-served to the States respectively, or to the people.' Some folks started trying to exercise these rights to the extreme and indeed Congress was getting mighty nervous when some states threatened to quit sending taxes to the feds and the last thing Congress wanted was a call for a Constitutional Convention. They knew that at such a Convention, anything could be submitted, not just the issue at hand. Believe me, the feds treated the States with a lot more respect and the door started swinging both ways.

"Speaking of the Constitution, Mr. Williams, I believe before your nap, there was a big flap about flag burning, wasn't there?"

"Indeed, there was and I'm curious as to what ever happened to that issue."

"Well, Hugh, a bill was tossed back and forth between the House and the Senate until both parties got sick of hearing about it so they stonewalled it and got it buried. You may be pleased to learn than many jurisdictions took the bull by the horns and in many parts of the U.S. today, the penalties are very severe for anyone stealing a flag and putting the torch to it. The powers that be merely made their arson laws much stronger and coupled with theft charges, flag burning is rare today as nobody wants to burn their own banner. The class of hoodlums that burn flags usually can't afford to purchase one.

"While we're on the subject of the Constitution, did you include the Fourth Amendment in your original questionnaire? I don't recall hearing it mentioned, so if it's alright with the group, I'd like to interject a little tid-bit at this time.

"Back in about 2010, many folks had had enough of the government trying to run their lives and decided to let the bureaucrats know who was paying the freight and who should be making the rules. The restaurant and bar owners nationwide signed petitions to the effect they would decide how their establishments would be run.

"Citing the provision in the Fourth Amendment pertaining to citizens' right to be secure in their persons, houses, papers and effects, they informed the local powers that be that henceforth, the *owners* would decide whether or not to allow smoking in their respective establishments. As it wasn't practical to arrest four million people, an important victory was won by the people and a constitutional crisis was averted. As many merchants opted for a no-smoking environment, there are still thousands of restaurants available for those that prefer that atmosphere. Bars and taverns *really* welcomed the choice.

"With that, I conclude my day in the saddle and apologize if it sounded more like preaching instead of teaching, but I have very strong feelings about the subject and, if anything, my brief research made me that much more patriotic and cognizant of just how fragile our freedoms are."

OVEREXPOSED

The U.S. Government's presence at the 1998 World Exposition in Lisbon, Portugal may have left taxpayers exposed to big bills. The State Department's Inspector General (IG) has uncovered some fiscal follies in the U.S. Expo '98 effort, which was headed up by former Congressman and Democratic Party consultant Tony Coelho. The IG found that Coelho opted to stay in a Lisbon Hotel rather than the $18,000 per month luxury apartment that was rented for him and that he spent $800 on a chauffeured Mercedes instead of using the Expo Commission's van fleet. He gave pay raises that netted Expo pavilion employees a 34%-200% increase without any documented justification, and put his niece on the payroll without proving the need to waive government anti-nepotism rules. The biggest budget boo-boo was Coelho's 'personal' $300,000 loan contracted with a private bank to fund a memorial built near the U.S. government's pavilion. But the IG says that taxpayers may be on the hook for the liability, unless private funds are raised to cover it. When the State Department began reviewing its participation in Expo 98, auditors thought the price tag would amount to $8 million. The actual amount was $9.8 million.

Capital Ideas
November/December 1999

CHAPTER 8

Okay, okay, I know it's my turn in the barrel" was the greeting received by the "contemporary, and not-so-contemporary," exchange of knowledge group at Resurrection Retirement Resort.

"Alright, where did I leave off?"

"You had just become the butt of a young Russian's joke," volunteered an older nurse from the front row.

"Oh yes, now it comes back to me," responded Mr. Williams. "We were on a boat ride on the Neva River in Leningrad.

"When we had inquired earlier at the Intourist Service Bureau regarding our rental car that was supposed to have been at the airport, we were told that we had to go to the Astoria Hotel to make arrangements. When I asked why we couldn't check by telephone, I was informed that this was impossible. They probably didn't want to admit that their phone service left a lot to be desired. The little experience I had with phones in Russia confirmed that.

"We went back to where we had started the boat trip and decided to hail a taxi. We later learned that this was not done in Russia. The taxis kept passing us by although many were empty. I walked over and asked a policeman where we could get a cab but he understood no English. He seemed to understand taxi as it is the same in Russian and he directed us to the other side of the street. Still they refused to pick us up even when I approached them while they were stopped for a red light. We later learned that taxis must be assigned and one had to go through channels.

Boys who helped us in Leningrad

"After a wait that must have been over an hour, we were approached by two young men who had been sitting on the seawall watching us.

"They asked for smoking tobacco so I gave them some cigarettes—I had that nasty habit in those days. They then asked where we wanted to go and we informed them that we were trying to get to the Astoria Hotel. It was then that we learned that it would be impossible to secure a taxi at that point. For first year English students they did quite well as they volunteered to lead us to where we could catch a bus. Much to our surprise, they boarded the bus with us and even paid our fare. While on the bus, they would speak only Russian and acted as though they didn't know us. Soon, they indicated it was time to get off. We couldn't figure why they had us get off at least six blocks short of our destination when the bus went right to the hotel. We soon discovered they wanted to talk, but as was the case with most Russians, they would not talk with Americans where anyone could hear.

"I wanted to ask them many questions, but they were so busy asking us questions I didn't get much of a chance. As it turned out, we learned more by their questions than we could possibly have learned from any answers they may have had to ours. Their inquiries were to be repeated many more times before we left the Soviet Union. Almost everywhere the questions were the same: 'Do you have an automobile? A colored TV? Do you own your own home? How much money do you make and how much did your clothes cost?' While they were very interested in our answers they, like many others, looked at us in disbelief. We thanked them for their courtesy, gave them our address and promised to send the pictures we had taken of them if they would write.

"We located the car rental agency of Intourist only to be confronted with a staff that spoke no English. They called someone from another office in the hotel and she saved the day. Through her, we learned we could not get a car on Sunday, but if we would return the next day at noon, they would have a car for us. We decided to return to our hotel and sought out transportation. Who did we draw for this assignment? You guessed it, our 'symphony Conductor'. It was at this time that I was thankful I had packed some tranquilizers for this trip. Because the City of Leningrad was built on many islands with hundreds of miles of waterways interlacing it, there are naturally hundreds of bridges. Leningrad was often referred to as the 'Venice of the North.' Many of those bridges were short high arches over the canals and when one crossed them at sixty miles per hour, one had to hold on to keep one's head from hitting the top of the automobile. The reaction in the stomach was not unlike that experienced on a roller coaster.

"Time out. Let's take a quick coffee break and now the ball is back in *your* court. I have been playing a little guessing game with myself trying to see if I can forecast what your next subject will be."

Some of the participants had started bringing pastries to these sessions so, along with the coffee, they could take a little nourishment. After a lot of chit-chat and second guessing as to what subject would be dealt with next, a middle-aged gentlemen, who had absolutely no connection with the rest home nor its staff, raised his hand and volunteered to give his spiel on politics and what he remembered had happened since way back in 2000. This man had visited a friend that was a resident of the institution and when he heard about the course in 'living history' he couldn't wait to participate. Introducing himself as Mason Paulson, he commenced:

"I admire the ambition of some of these young folks that are taking the time to research various subjects so they can fill in the blanks for you but I have been blessed with a photographic memory and because politics has always been my avocation, I can probably bring you up to date both from memory and from many articles written on the subject. In the last twenty years, there have probably been more changes in American politics than there had been in the previous fifty years.

"Although most of the media and, indeed, many of the syndicated writers finally came to their senses, they hated to admit it, but there were groups in America that were attempting to use our freedoms to *destroy* our freedoms. When they delved into the inner workings of some of the environmental groups, they were shocked to discover that many of those that wielded power in those groups couldn't care less about clean water, endangered species and pollution in general. They had but one goal and that was to destroy capitalism. The newspapers, TV, radio and all other forms of communication suddenly woke up to the fact that some of the very movements they had been championing were merely socialist, if not outright communist, and the press and broadcast media would be the first to feel the effects should some of these idiots ever gain real power.

"Speaking of environmental groups or environmental nuts as some referred to them, some of the extreme fringe cells, such as the ELF—Earth Liberation Front—finally went too far with their wanton destruction of other peoples' property and the defecation hit the oscillation. When some of the perpetrators of those arson attacks were brought to justice, it was common for them to receive sentences longer than some received for murder.

"It was after the elections in the year 2000 that the general public began to get more educated about what the parties and individual candidates stood for. Perhaps it was the smooch planted on his wife at the Democratic National Convention by then-Vice President Al Gore that precipitated the sudden interest in 'who's minding the store?' When women were heard to say they voted for Al because of the way he kissed his wife a few folks started to become concerned about our two Party system. A few, jokingly, remarked that perhaps we made a mistake way back in 1920 when we passed the 21st Amendment. Come to think of it, that was exactly 100 years ago. My, doesn't time fly when you're having fun?

"Soon, old-fashioned town halls sprang up all over the country. The American Legion, VFW, civic and fraternal organizations soon tried to outdo one another in the field of political education. Most of these organizations insisted that these town-hall meetings be strictly neutral and could and would consist of teaching, not preaching. Perhaps the biggest surprise to many was the fact that even the labor unions wanted to get into the act. It was revealed that many organizations that masqueraded as 'dogooders' were potential enemies for if they were successful in bringing down capitalism union jobs would soon go down the gurgler.

"It seemed rather incongruous for labor and management to be sleeping in the same bed but both sides realized which side their bread was buttered on and as a team, no extremist groups were about to pull their rug. Schools were soon clamoring for little pocket-sized copies of the Declaration Of Independence and the Constitution. At first some printing firms started a bidding war as to who would supply them, but it didn't take long for advertisers to recognize their value and soon every school in the country, both public and private, had those little books. Nobody had the heart to tell folks that the Chinese used the same method way back in the late sixties but, of course, Mao sang a much different tune.

"I should also point out, that the 2000 election really brought home the fact that when it came to voting, most Americans couldn't care less. While more and more people voted, due probably to the absentee voting process, the majority sat on their hands. It was this wholesale lack of interest that no doubt prompted the formation of a new party consisting mostly of independents, but swelled by the ranks of those who identified themselves as conservatives along with many, many so-called Southern Democrats. I'll have to give the organizers credit; they didn't mention the word conservative for the democrats and their bleeding-heart liberal friends in the news media had used a wide brush to paint conservatives with broad radical strokes. You could ask the average 'Joe Sixpak' on the street ten questions and his answers could prove, beyond a doubt, he was a conservative, but to him, it was a naughty word.

"Of course, any new party had one hell of a time getting any recognition but that struggling group claimed the high ground and held it. While there were literally thousands of names suggested for the new party, the ultimate choice was both obvious and simple. It adopted the name of the Common Sense Party and championed one main objective: *accountability*. It was but a few years before the remnants of the Perot movement came on board and, lo and behold, they started getting a few candidates elected at city, county and even state levels. They had the good sense not to try to take on either Congress or the White House while just coming out of the starting blocks.

"Most folks claimed they didn't have a prayer, but when members of the two large existing parties started introducing legislation that was right from the Common Sense Party's platform, people started to sit up and take notice. Nothing really humongous, you understand, but every plank introduced and ultimately passed, certainly firmed up the foundation of the fledgling party. They really got a lot of ink when they called America's attention to the fact that many states required no proof of citizenship and illegal immigrants were casting votes that, in some instances, tilted the outcome in some contests.

"Former President Bush got legislation passed to the effect that all voters henceforth would be required to show proof of citizenship prior to the election of 2012. While it is still possible to use forgeries and the like, it greatly reduced the practice of illegals voting and indeed, it sent some of those undocumented characters home.

"Around the year 2000, you may recall there was a rash of forged credit cards, driver's licenses and the like. One magazine even advertised a firm that would give you a new social security number so you could obtain credit again even while bankrupt. To some this was the last straw and Senator Smythe Gordon from Oregon introduced, and got passed, legislation to the effect that anyone caught with more than one social security number, except, of course, a legitimate loss of same, would be prohibited from collecting on any account. Of course this had little effect on the younger generation because we all know they 'live forever,' but it did cause many to have second thoughts.

"A side benefit was a rider to Senator Gordon's bill offered by Senator Craig Lawrence of Idaho to the effect that Americans would no longer be required to give out their social security numbers to anyone other than the Internal Revenue and any institutions that reported to same. Most folks were under the impression that this was already the law of the land, but when they complained to their congressional representatives, their words fell on deaf ears.

"No longer could one be denied credit for refusal to divulge this information. The credit reporting agencies had a cow, but Uncle Sam informed them they would have to come up with their own numbering system and that the U.S. Government was not going to be a party to supplying them with a master file. No, this wasn't done for vindictiveness, but because so many forgeries were taking place and the fact that a few shrewd operators could literally mortgage somebody's home if he knew his victim's social security number.

"The new party started growing in popularity and soon they were picking up offices all over the land. A city council seat here, a county commissioner there and, would you believe it, even a few seats in the U.S House of Representatives? Of course, they wielded little power, but they made big news when they tried to get legislation past the various committees. They pulled an old Ronald Reagan trick; they took their cause to the people. If the hue and cry became loud enough, their suggestions would suddenly show up with a major party member's name on it. I'll have to hand it to those pioneers of that new movement. Instead of copying failures from all over the world, they copied success. They repeated Ronald Reagan's words to the effect that 'Anything is possible if you don't care who gets the credit.'

"Shortly after making its first inroads in our nation's capital, Common Sense made headlines, it was they who proposed changing Veterans Day to Election Day. November 11 no longer had the significance it once had as we no longer have a surviving veteran of the First World War. Changing Veterans Day was a lot easier than the other way around for that would have required a Constitutional Amendment. This legislation was soon enacted, but it proved to be a hollow victory as the vast majority of Americans now vote by mail and even e-mail. The combination of these circumstances eliminated the squabbles about results being announced in the eastern time zone prior to the closing of the polls in the west. One of the pledges taken by new party members said, in so many words, that you believed in what was good for the nation, not any individual nor political party.

"Normally, it would take years for a minor party to make even a dent in the system that America had lived with for so many years. Having so many disenchanted voters coupled with a larger and larger field of independents plus the influence and money of a billionaire like Ross Perot was probably what led to the success of his new party in the 90s. Those folks at least proved it could be done. The Common Sense Party kept harping on one subject and it soon became the byword in government at all levels: accountability, accountability, accountability.

"The party charged that, for years, we had been governed by fiat. They would stand up and shout: 'Show me in the Constitution where it says we have to preserve wetlands by taking land away from our citizens; where does it say we must set aside 2,000 acres for a pair of birds to breed? Where does it say we can't build roads in wilderness areas to aid in fighting fires? Where does it say we must protect one species at the expense of another?'

"This was just the tip of the iceberg, and folks finally started questioning legislation at all levels. When one Common Sense candidate gave a speech on national TV, it probably did more than anything else to bring home his party's point. He pointed out that the average American will put a buck into a soft-drink machine and when the beverage is not dispensed, he will kick the machine, rock it, pound on it, threaten to sue and sometimes go into a rage but he lets the government reach into his pocket every payday, extract one-third of his earnings and not even question where it goes and how it's spent.

"The party borrowed another suggestion from former President Reagan. They were able to convince a large manufacturer to let them conduct an experiment with their several hundred employees. They set up a series of kiosks in a row near the exit from the factory. Come payday, they paid their employees in cash…the complete gross amount. The employees were then required to go through the line of kiosks, depositing funds at every stop. To the workers, taxes, social security, etc. were just some figures that a computer printed on their check stub, but when they actually had their gross pay in hand and were forced to fork over, in many cases hundreds of dollars, the point was really driven home. I do believe if every employer in America had tried this experiment there would have been a revolution.

"The Common Sense Party has really changed the political scene, here in this country, even at the lower echelons of government. Some states now have laws that say for every new bill passed in their respective legislatures, two bills have to be repealed. Some states had literally thousands of new bills presented each session and some folks predict that in those states that adopted the new 'two for one' rule, their state codes may be manageable by the next millennium. That's a joke but just might be true. Some states have now copied Nebraska and have adopted the concept of a unicameral legislature. There have been many more innovations, brought about largely by the new Party, but I may be stepping on somebody else's toes so if they're not covered in their reports, I'll be back."

"Let's give this fellow a big hand. While I wasn't aware of all these incidents he has described, he certainly *must* have either a photographic memory or a vivid imagination. Indeed, I think many of you may have missed your callings. Perhaps you should all consider a career in writing."

DIRT POOR

Even in the computer age, "Appalachia" continues to conjure up images of unemployed adults and malnourished children living in shacks. Well, now we know at least one reason why. The federal Appalachian Regional Commission (ARC) was designed to award economic development grants to poor rural communities in thirteen states. But the commission's definition of 'poor rural community' is an interesting one as an Associated Press investigation recently uncovered. One of the largest recipients of ARC grants is the city of Pittsburgh, (yes, the one in Pennsylvania), netting $70.4 million over the last three decades. Spartanburg, SC, which made Money Magazine's list of "booming locales" was apparently busted enough to receive a $5 million ARC Check that helped build sewer lines for luxury automaker BMW's factory there.

Other giveaways included $500,000 for road access improvements to a Pennsylvania Amusement Park and $75,200 for an Alabama town's bronze tribute to track star Jesse Owens. High taxes and misdirected federal aid are probably more responsible than anything else for Appalachia's unending misery but Washington's shrill-bullies have shouted down any rational debate over ARC's usefulness.

Capital Ideas
November/December 1999

CHAPTER 9

Monday morning was absolutely picture perfect like an old poem that said: *October's Bright Blue Weather*. Hugh Williams looked more rested than he had appeared during any of the previous sessions and seemed eager to proceed with his "history lesson." "I sincerely hope you are as anxious to hear more about the former Soviet Union as I am about sharing my experiences with you.

"You may recall I related to you the experience my wife and I had in our attempt to secure our rental car in Leningrad. Please excuse me, I know it's now known as St. Petersburg, but I am trying to convey my story in the context of the time in which it occurred.

"After our break-neck ride from the Astoria Hotel back to the Leningrad Hotel we immediately headed to the tenth floor and, would you believe it, we were advised that we would be fed in the first floor dining room as a large group had reserved the tenth-floor facilities. We were seated with a gentleman from Scotland who was en-route to Estonia to visit his eighty-four-year-old mother. He told us he had to wait for nineteen months for his visa. It seemed that if you indicated on your visa application that you wish to visit a Soviet citizen, you could plan on a year and a half delay in obtaining your visa.

"We ordered beef stroganoff and it was surprisingly tasteful. I even tackled the red caviar but am still convinced that it was better steel-head bait than food. The decor in the dining room and nightclub on the lower level would compare with most anything in the West. The dining room was actually on the second floor with a large circular staircase leading down to the dance floor, which was surrounded by tables. The orchestra pit was a balcony suspended about halfway between the two levels. We couldn't believe our ears when we heard the orchestra play a jazzed-up version of 'Ramona' followed by 'Ave Maria'. There were many Russians there that evening, including a party of naval officers and their ladies. It seemed rather incongruous to see them do the Monkey and the Crawl. The Russians really dug rock and roll and even their radio stations featured their own version of that music. After a nightcap at the International Club on the ninth floor, we headed for our room. Watching so many service men and their girlfriends walking along the seawall in nearly broad daylight made it hard to convince ourselves it was after midnight.

"It was at this time that I decided to start a journal on the Soviet Union by putting our experiences on tape. I must admit I was a little hesitant, as earlier in the evening, I had been warned by the Scotsman as well as a tour guide from Finland that tape recorders were a no-no. Because of this, Winnie decided to keep a brief handwritten diary in case my recorder and/or tapes were confiscated.

"After breakfast on Monday morning, we devoted some time to writing post cards before taking a taxi back to the Astoria Hotel. Again, another wild ride with the radio turned up full blast, This time at the rental agency we did not have the benefit of an interpreter, but the staff recognized me from the day before. I presented my voucher and they filled out a long form written in English as well as in Russian. When they asked for our passports, I suddenly had that sinking feeling. Yes, they were still at the desk at the Leningrad Hotel.

"Once again, a wild ride, this time courtesy of Intourist to retrieve our passports. This was just too much for Winnie so she opted to remain at our hotel rather than endure another round trip across town. She pleaded with me to abandon the whole idea but I couldn't back out now. Just the fact that Intourist was not noted for issuing refunds was enough to entice me to see that I received my ninety-three rubles worth.

"Back at the Astoria Hotel, after reading the rental contract carefully to assure myself that it covered insurance, I signed on the dotted line. They issued me four tickets good for forty liters of gasoline then accompanied me to the parking lot to acquaint me with the nomenclature of the vehicle all in sign language. I had quite an audience for this procedure and I never will know what they all thought was so funny.

"When I finally drove away, I must admit I was a bit nervous. They claimed there were relatively few automobiles in the Soviet Union so they must have all been on the same streets I was driving on. With so many squares, circles, monuments and fountains, I found myself with traffic converging on all directions. By this time, of course, I knew my way back to our hotel like a native and my only difficulty was when I stopped for pedestrians. They didn't do that in Russia so folks in cars behind me leaned on their horns and policemen blew their whistles. How they kept from killing more people than they did, I'll never know. I must admit, however, they were way ahead of us in posting international drivers symbols, most of which were self-explanatory.

"Arriving back at the hotel, I drove around to the back where they had a new parking lot. The girl attendant charged me three kopecks to park but as she spoke no English, I was unable to determine if this was for an hour or a day. To get from the parking lot into the hotel involved a walk of three blocks. Hotels in Russia had no back doors and, as at the airport, in spite of the fact they had several sets of doors in front, only half of one door was open at any one time. We were told that this enabled the authorities to keep better track of the guests and the doormen inside and outside were members of the secret police. There was no way to confirm this, but it did seem logical.

"We decided to drive out to the Summer Palace of the Czars, which was located on the Baltic Sea about twenty-five miles from the city. I suggested that I get the car and pick up Winnie at the front door of the hotel When I walked into the parking lot, there was a man waiting for me. He kept gesturing to me and pointed to a new red car parked near the entrance to the lot. I thought he was trying to tell me to park there when I returned so I nodded in agreement. He started yelling and waving his arms as I tried to ease out of the lot. He ran along side of the car finally reaching in and turning off the ignition. I was about half mad and half scared when another man approached and started jabbering as loudly as the first man. I finally understood one word: Astoria. It was then that I began to get the idea they wanted me to go back to the Astoria Hotel.

"The first man got into the car and the second followed in the little red car. I knew that, by this time, Winnie was probably getting concerned and I will never forget the expression on her face when she saw me driving up with a Russian man in the front seat. I explained to her what I thought was taking place and decided to let the Russian do the driving. When we arrived at the Astoria, we had a delegation waiting for us. Someone who spoke a smattering of English somehow conveyed the message they had rented us the wrong car. I refused to surrender the car, however, until my papers had been changed. I couldn't help but notice one of the men had a screwdriver and was changing the license plates. While the red car was much smaller than the first car we had, it was much newer with only about 3,000 on the odometer. They told us the first one was a Moskvich and the newer car was a Kiev produced by the new factory that was recently opened by Fiat.

Again, the instructions as to the function of every control on the automobile and we were off to the summer palace."

"Okay fellow historians, remind me where we left off…en-route from the Astoria Hotel to the Summer Palace of the Czars…So who is our next guest lecturer?" One of the receptionists, Trudy Jade, from the front office and who was fudging on her coffee break stood up and announced:

Russian rental car…Soviet Fiat

"You know, I had never taken an interest in anything except making a living, keeping up my apartment and enjoying an occasional movie with a date now and again, but these sessions have sparked a curiosity that I didn't know existed. So with your kind permission, I'd like to put in my two cents worth. Suppose I pick up where the last gentleman left off. Thank goodness he left a little for me to elaborate on.

"I knew very little about party politics and never even bothered to vote but I read an article a few years ago that is just now beginning to make sense. I believe it was a warning about just how fragile our Republic has become. It pointed out how Hitler came to power nearly one hundred years ago by starting out with just a few followers in a beer hall. The article went on to say that if that madman could accomplish such a feat in those relatively primitive times, what's to stop a similar incident in this day of computers, faxes and the like? The author attributed the rapid rise of the Common Sense Party to our modern, lightning-fast communications and commented that we are indeed fortunate that the goals of the new party were nothing like those of Hitler.

"A previous speaker really hit home with me when he gave the analogy of the fellow that inserted the dollar in the soft-drink dispenser and received no beverage. When we talk about a dollar, most of us can relate to it, but when you start referring to billions, it's beyond our comprehension. I recall that over the years, when I did glance at a newspaper or catch a TV newscast, how angry I'd become when we were told about the national budget. Most of us merely accepted the figures, which now run in the trillions. Whenever the subject arose concerning foreign aid, over coffee, the response was always the same. Charity begins at home. Some folks started asking just where does that money go? We knew that if our Rotary Club donated funds to fight polio or purify a village's water supply the funds got into the hands of the ordinary man. When our church filled a steamship container with clothing, we had reason to believe those garments would go to the poor. When Uncle Sugar doled out billions, who got it? I understand it ended up in the hands of the bankers and precious little sifted down to the needy.

"One case that was cited took place in your day, Mr. Williams. We gave $5 billion to Israel and they spent $3 billion in France purchasing Mirage fighters. This stuck in the craw of many folks and the results finally came to fruition in the form of a bill introduced and passed by the Common Sense Party. That bill said, in so many words, that 'Any foreign aid deemed necessary shall be in the form of vouchers or credits redeemable only in the United States.' Will wonders never cease? Would you believe that after many years and billions of dollars, it finally occurred to somebody that we could actually produce American jobs through our generosity?

"Another sore spot with folks for many years was the extravagance of our federal government when it came to purchasing goods and services. Mr. Williams, you may recall all the hula baloo about the $600 toilet seats, the $1,000 hammers and the $7,000 coffeepots. In fact, wasn't it in about 2000 that we read about the Post Office Department spending around $248,000 dollars to move a couple of employees about fifty miles? Was anything ever done about those abuses? No way.

"Not so today. It's taken nearly twenty years, but the federal government no longer has hundreds of accounting systems where no CPA firm can get a handle on expenditures. Indeed, there used to be literally billions of dollars in the pipelines of the various agencies and nobody had the foggiest idea of how much had been spent, nor did anyone seem to give a damn. Let me assure you they give more than a damn now for some of the folks who had been so quick to sign requisitions for unneeded items at ridiculous prices are now walking down the street talking to themselves. In addition, any firm caught deliberately ripping off the government, not only has to make restitution, they are absolutely forbidden to even submit a bid to the government for five years. Funny, but the government's cost of doing business has taken a dramatic downward turn.

"We haven't solved all the problems, by any means, but we are making a dent in them. One of the biggest problems is still the 'underground 'economy. It has been estimated that the government is losing close to half a trillion dollars annually due to the huge increase in bartering. While we are ever closer to a cash-less society and unless goods are exchanged for other goods, it is more difficult to do business under the table. Audits have shown merchandise either in inventory or removed from inventory with no commensurate increase nor decrease in net worth and has resulted in some pretty hefty penalties.

"It was also revealed way back in your days in the nineties, that an estimated six million individuals and firms never filed a tax return. You can bet your sweet bippy those folks were hiding in 2000 and 2010 when the census people came calling. Something encouraging did happen while you were napping, however. You're probably not going to believe this, but some members of the Common Sense Party actually dug up and dusted off the old Grace Commission Report and if it showed how much could have been saved way back in 1990, you can imagine the savings we are enjoying today. With that, I can't wait to get back to Leningrad," concluded Trudy.

"Thanks so much, Trudy, for your fine update. I was so glad to learn so many things I had hoped for before my accident actually transpired. Guess there's hope for our Republic after all. I recall a line from somewhere in English Lit to the effect that: 'murder will out'; so I wonder if we're presumptuous if we say, 'Common Sense will prevail.' A little play on words there. I can still recall a joke that was making the rounds clear back in the sixties. It seems a little kid in Ohio wrote a letter to Santa Claus explaining that he had no father and his mother was sick so would Santa please send him a hundred dollars so they could have a Christmas? The letter naturally ended up in the dead-letter office in Washington, D.C. where a postal worker felt sorry for the little kid, stuck a five-dollar bill in an envelope and mailed it to the Ohio address. A couple of weeks later, another letter from the same kid showed up at the dead-letter office and it read: Thanks for the money, Santa, but please don't send any more via Washington, D.C.; those bastards took ninety-five dollars out of it.

"Yes, I know, it's an oldie, but I still think it's a goody."

SOUR-CLOUT

It's bad enough that special interests have lobbyists hoping to pick our pockets for federal hand-outs, but what happens when the 'special interest' is a state or local government? A recent investigation by Gannett News Service has discovered that some of the biggest money-grabbers on Capitol Hill are the very same governments that grab your money through property taxes, sales taxes and excises.

The Pennsylvania Turnpike Commission, for example, spends $300,000 every year for a Washington DC lobbying firm to shake down federal transportation appropriators for more highway funds. So did Hawaii, which spent $250,000 to retain the high-powered firm of Vemer-Lipfert to secure more road money. Monroe County, NY spent local tax dollars to pressure federal Rep. Louise Slaughter (D). who represents that area, to give up her opposition to a $1.5 million Congressional sop for a freshwater cooling system. The fact that Mississippi officials have Senate Majority Leader Trent Lott (R-MS) on their side didn't stop them from paying $100,000 to a lobbyist working to steer defense dollars to the Magnolia State. All told, lower-level governments spent $34.3 million in taxpayer dollars in 1995 to hit up Uncle Sam for...well, for more taxpayers' dollars.

Capital Ideas
January/February 2000

CHAPTER 10

"How's everyone this fine day?" questioned 'Professor' Williams, as his ever enlarging audience finished their morning coffee and took their seats. "You all look bright-eyed and bushy-tailed and if this keeps up, we're going to have to rent an auditorium. And, as for you Dr. Laurel, I've noticed that you have been keeping extensive notes so please remember I have the movie rights," he commented and laughed.

"No, folks, you don't have to remind me where I left off in Russia. My memory seems to improve with every passing day. Has someone been spiking my coffee with that new-fangled drug that's supposed to combat memory loss? I've never felt better in my life and while I'm not ready to run a marathon, as we used to say, I'm not as good as I was once, but I'm as good once as I ever was."

Hugh Williams leaned over and almost whispered to some of the nurses in the front row whose complexions had turned rosy with that last remark. He apologized by saying "I'm not coming on to you, ladies, I was merely trying to convey the message that I'm not a candidate for Viagra.

"Meanwhile, back at the ranch...uh...I mean Leningrad All I knew was the general direction, but I drove to the Summer Palace of the

Czars as if I had driven there several times.

"This had to be one of the most beautiful sights in Russia with so much ornate gold work, the statues and the fountains. We walked all the way down a canal, which stretches from the front of the palace to the Baltic Sea.

"There we discovered we could have taken a

Summer Palace of the Czars

hydra-foil from downtown, a thirty-minute trip compared to the hour or more it took us to drive. The grounds would have been even more enjoyable were it not for the unbearable heat.

Canal from summer palace to Baltic Sea

"We did discover, however, that Russians made the most delicious ice cream we had ever tasted and a serving helped us cool off a little.

"Fortunately, many of the signs on the Palace grounds were in English as well as Russian which helped to make us more appreciative of Russian history. Looking at such grandeur and

Purchasing Russian ice cream

wealth one can almost understand why there was a revolution. What a pity it only transferred that wealth, along with the power, from one oppressive government to another which was even worse. It was then owned by the people but the people were still very poor by our standards.

"We arrived back at our hotel about seven in the evening. After dinner, we decided to try the night bar in the basement. It also turned out to be a Western currency bar where the best Scotch Whisky and American cigarettes were available. A Russian naval man was talking to me in Pidgin English and enjoying a drink when two men, dressed in civilian clothes, came in and escorted him away. They talked for some time in the foyer and eventually let him go. I can only surmise what had taken place but it tended to confirm our earlier suspicions. We had been told repeatedly by experienced travelers that the Soviet Union was on the horns of a dilemma; they desperately wanted foreign currency but were afraid of foreign contact with their citizens. Aside from that incident, we enjoyed ourselves very much talking with tourists from all over the world. We retired a little early considering the fact the bar remained open until four in the morning.

"After breakfast on Tuesday, I went to Intourist to see if they had been able to secure the private guide I had requested. They had, and after payment of ten rubles I was instructed to meet her at ten o'clock. Her name was Natasha and she spoke English very well. She admitted she would be working under a handicap as she was used to just talking and leaving the driving up to a bus driver. Even with her giving directions, we became lost a couple of times.

"At one stop, the transmission of the car stuck in fourth gear. Fortunately I was able to nurse it back to the Astoria Hotel. Natasha was able to explain our difficulties and they promised to have it fixed within the hour. At this time, our tour became a walking tour through the huge St Isaacs cathedral.

"The icons were fantastic and we were amazed at Natasha's knowledge of the Bible and Christianity. I asked her about this and she explained that it was a requirement for her work. She was quick to add, however, 'I do not believe…no one can make me believe.' I remarked that it sounded as if someone was forcing her *not* to believe, but she missed the point.

"I told her that I had always been under the impression that under communism everyone was equal with no discrimination. She answered in the affirmative so I complained about how we had been treated as individuals compared to tour groups and this had left us with a very bad impression. She apologized but could offer no excuse. I asked about their alleged classless society and she came unglued. 'Of course we have classes. You surely wouldn't classify a peasant as being equal to an artisan.' I muttered something about restudying Marx, and

St. Isaacs Cathedral in Leningrad

80

Building from which Lenin led the Revolution

let it go at that.

"We walked back to our car-rental agency and our car was ready for us. They explained that I shouldn't rest my hand on the gear shift knob and jam it through the gears as we did back home. They also showed me how to get the ignition turned on when it locked as it had several times previously. I was beginning to get a little nervous about the vehicle, as it seemed so delicate.

"Obviously our guide had been well indoctrinated along the communist line. She had pat answers for every question. When I asked her how many people worked for the government, her answer was 'everybody.' She gave quite a spiel regarding her right to a secret ballot and the wonderful representation each citizen had in his government.

"One of the buildings on the tour was the one from which Lenin directed the revolution.

"Natasha explained that he had been disguised as a wounded laborer, wrapped in bandages and smuggled into the structure. After a picture taking session in front of this edifice, we returned to the car to find several men looking it over. It seemed those cars were still a novelty to the Russians and they were very curious as to why an American was driving a Soviet automobile. Through Natasha, they asked me what I thought of it. I just shrugged my shoulders. Later I told Natasha that I didn't want to hurt their feelings by giving them my honest opinion. Her reply was: 'That's alright, I told them.' When I asked her what she said, she answered, 'I told them it was no damn good, just like everything else made in this country.'

"I didn't have to tell her we thought the weather was hot. She volunteered that 'it was the worst heat wave since 1917.' Good,' I said, 'does that mean there is going to be another revolution?' Evidently she failed to see the humor in this remark, as her expression told me that I hadn't won any brownie points.

"Upon completion of the tour, we returned to the hotel as I had advised them that we would check out by one o'clock. The service bureau of Intourist had already issued us coupons for our hotels in Novgorod, Moscow. Novosibirsk, Irkutsk and Khabarovsk along with special coupons for breakfasts and sightseeing tours in each city. Evidently, if there were restrictions against Americans traveling east of the Volga, it had not filtered down through the bureaucracy to the lower echelons. However, I was still apprehensive as we had been told we would obtain our railroad tickets in Moscow."

"Batter up! Who's next up to the plate?" asked 'Professor'" Williams. "What are you going to lay on us this fine day? Or should I say lay on me, as most of you have lived through what I am just learning?" With this a young man, who introduced himself as Henry Dodge and looked like he should be playing for the NFL, stepped forward.

"Mr. Williams, if it's alright with you and your students, I'm a Political Science major at WSU and between what I remember and what I have studied, I may be able to shed some light on the subject of employment.

"They tell me you were rendered unconscious sometime in the year 2000. You were aware then that our economy had been booming and both the government and the populace were spending money like there was no tomorrow. Unfortunately, not too long before the elections of 2000, the country started experiencing a slow down. Much of this was attributed to the continued slowdown of the Far Eastern markets coupled with an increase in the value of the Euro. Some economists pegged the starting date of Clinton's recession as the day he declared war on Bill Gates. It was said that if Clinton had spent a fraction of the time and money he expended pursuing Microsoft on the pursuit of Osama bin Laden, 9/11 might never have happened.

"The result was a lowering of interest rates by the fed and subsequent demand by other nations to redeem their bonds they had purchased and which had given a rather unstable foundation to our prosperity. Shades of 1929? Well, not quite. You may remember from your history lessons that much of the really negative effect of the stock market crash of 1929 was exacerbated by the Smoot-Hawley Tariff Bill. This was a vain attempt to create more American jobs by placing high tariffs on foreign imports. The other nations retaliated and, as America was the world's largest producing nation in those days, our economy really went south. This time, however, the shoe was on the other foot. America was now the world's largest consuming nation and similar legislation enacted around 2009 had the opposite effect of Smoot-Hawley. The producing nations of the world weren't about to cut off their largest market. Some side effects, of course, were the increase in the cost of living and a decrease in the balance, or lack thereof, in the foreign trade deficit. At long last, America subjected imports to the same quality tests as were being demanded of our products being sold in their countries Finally we were close to playing on a level field.

"It was about this time that America finally woke up to the fact that NAFTA was a mistake and indeed, some could hear the big swooshing sound of our jobs going south much like Perot had predicted. Such a plan worked in Europe as there was not the big difference in the economies of that continent that exist in the Western Hemisphere. Uncle Sam told his neighbors if they insist on taking our jobs, they were not to be rewarded by taking our money. Stiff tariffs on goods produced by American firms outside our borders had the effect of discouraging the outward migration of industry.

"The average Joe Sixpak can't relate to figures in the billions, but many of them could observe that when they drove across the Mexican border, they were, more or less, forced to purchase Mexican insurance. This, in spite of the fact their American policies stated their coverage was good in all of North America. When an American was involved in even a little fender bender, south of the border, he was frequently thrown in jail with an exorbitant bail. The sale of Mexican insurance was nothing short of outright extortion.

"If the playing field was to be level under NAFTA, the United States had to force Mexicans to purchase American insurance at the border. You can't believe how fast the Mexican government announced that henceforth, they would honor the provisions of American insurance policies.

"It was about this time that the average American citizen became aware of the fact that thousands, if not millions of our jobs were going bye-bye and they couldn't believe that ISPs—Internet Service Providers—were outsourcing most of their jobs to countries such as India. We really found out the power of the internet as millions of us got online and e-mailed everyone on our mail list and the message was sent: bring back our jobs or we will bring you down. Some firms chose to ignore the warning and they are no longer with us.

"Within the ranks of the unemployed, there was a great hue and cry for make-work projects. Unlike the CCC, WPA and other experiments of the thirties, people wanted more for the country than more campgrounds and hiking trails. What was needed was dignified work that would benefit the most people. Many of the unemployed, though skilled in many areas, had to be retrained along with those who possessed no skills at all.

"Congress set a goal of completely rewiring America putting all electric and telephone service underground. We started with cities like Miami and Charleston and gave first priorities to other cities with hurricane histories. Next we concentrated on cities such as Buffalo and other cities with heavy snowfalls. Soon it was the turn for all cities and villages in so-called tornado alley.

"This was quite a shock to many that had held down office jobs but the worst discomfort was the blisters they now had on their hands. The beauty of this program was the fact that the whole project required very little skill and the participants could be on the job within a couple of weeks. Most were employed operating the trenchers that dug the ditches and pulling wires through the newly laid conduits. Unlike programs tried back in the thirties, many of these projects actually paid for themselves after just a few hurricanes, blizzards and tornadoes.

"Naturally many folks opted for welfare, but, much to their chagrin, the Common Sense Party had been successful in pushing through legislation that decreed that all able-bodied recipients of these programs would be put to work guarding our schools, parks and public buildings. Armed with only walkie-talkies and a cell phone that could be used for calling 911 only, we couldn't believe how the vandalism rate plunged, Here was another case where a government program more than paid for itself.

"With the sharp decline in employment, the government naturally experienced a sharp decrease in the amount of revenue they could generate. They had no choice but to go on a diet and many government employees were forced to seek employment elsewhere. Those campaigning and recruiting members for Common Sense realized their party was too new and too fragile to offer some of their solutions to the government's dilemma. It was several years before they dared to suggest what was to become the biggest government reduction in the history of the nation. They started out slowly so as not to rock the boat. They suggested and got passed legislation that consolidated Post Offices and cut the number of Postmasters in half. I don't believe any of us realized that there were over 32,000 Postmasters, plus another 8,000 managers in smaller areas that report to those postmasters, in the United States at that time. Mercifully, these reductions were achieved strictly by attrition.

"Common Sense waited until their party was on a firmer foundation and their position in the political hierarchy was solidified before they came up with the most dramatic cost-cutting scheme in history. They pointed out that in the first hundred years or so in our history, some county lines were determined by the fact that every citizen within that county had to be able to reach the county seat by a half days' horse and buggy ride. That was fine until the advent of the automobile and eventually the Interstate Highway system. Now, we're asked, 'Does it make sense for a medium-sized state like Iowa to keep maintaining 99 counties? Think of it, 99 Court Houses, 99 sheriffs, 99 Boards of County Commissioners, 99 treasurers, and ad infinitum…Think of the duplication and overlapping occurring every day. If the number of these counties was reduced, even by half, the cost of government would be reduced by billions. Naturally, this required a real hard sell and even the assurance that most employee reductions would be by attrition; the plan met with stiff opposition.

"Some of the pioneers in the plan turned out to be cities instead of counties; the State of Washington has so many twin cities they defy logic. The powers that be figured if this new plan was so efficient at the county level, shouldn't the same logic apply at the city consolidation level? Slowly, but surely, some counties began to hold joint meetings with neighboring counties, for it was only natural that counties, like nations, were not anxious to relinquish their sovereignty. Well, we still have a long way to go, but one doesn't have to be a rocket scientist to realize the savings if America's 3,042 counties, boroughs and parishes were reduced by about half.

"I think it has been mentioned that the stock market started heading south in the 4th quarter of 2000. As the recession deepened, about the only bright spot in the economy was the housing industry. In the latter part of 2007, even that slowed down. Oh, there was still a lot of re-fi business, but that required not much more than paper shufflers when we desperately needed to put carpenters, plumbers, electricians and the like back to work.

"A few years later the president pushed a plan that was adopted by all agencies involved, including the IRS. Recognizing that the first waves of 'baby boomers' were starting to show up in the ranks of the retired, the president came up with a brilliant idea. He proposed that at the age of seventy and one-half, when those with IRAs and the like were forced to start withdrawing their funds, they could receive more than what was scheduled, with the provision the funds be gifted to children and/or grandchildren to be used only for the down payment on a home.

"This was a blessing for the retirees as these funds were tax-free and it started a mini-boom in the home construction industry. The government had an ulterior motive, however, as it accomplished two objectives. It put a lot of people to work and Uncle Sugar collected tax on the gifted funds from the recipients and at a much higher rate than he would have realized from most of the retirees.

"It was about this time, that many farmers marched on their respective capitols to demand the right to employ youngsters again to help harvest certain crops. They argued that it was stupid to restrict the use of twelve-year olds to pick berries because of chemicals used in the fields, while our schools were buying crops from countries that were still using dangerous pesticides. Also, some of our farmers were cited for employing illegal aliens with doctored documents. Putting younger kids back in the fields, helps keep some of them out of trouble and many are now able to buy some of their own school clothes.

"There have been other innovations in the field of employment, but like many of your subjects—many of them either dovetail or over-lap—I don't want to encroach on the next speaker's presentation. I happened to meet him for a cocktail last night and I know whereof I speak. Thank you so much for your kind indulgence."

MEATHEADS

Have you "herd" about the federal government's latest agricultural subsidy? It's left the U.S. Department of Agriculture (USDA) with a serious case of hoof-in-mouth disease. Thanks to the bison price support program, the USDA spent some $6 million of your money last year to buy up surplus buffalo meat that consumers refused to corral for their own kitchens. The federally funded blow-out represented 1/4 of all ground buffalo meat production in America and cost $3.45 per pound; more than many cuts of beefsteak on weekly specials at local supermarkets.

And guess who's singing "Dough on the Range" louder than any singing cowboy would dare? None other than billionaire bison own-er and Time-Warner Vice Chairman, Ted Turner, the single largest holder of shaggies in North America, with 17,000 head. The program has survived despite public ridicule that stopped similar price props for cheese and other commodities.

Capital Ideas
January/February 2000

CHAPTER 11

"Another day, another dollar in the hole…at least for you poor working stiffs" was the salutation that awaited those eager protégé 's of Hugh Williams this dark and drizzly day. It was the kind of day that made many of the participants *want* to spend the entire day in 'class'. Unfortunately many of them had a battle on their hands; they had to fight poverty.

"So what transpired when Winnie and I checked out of the Leningrad Hotel? While standing at the check out desk, I was asked by the clerk what time I would be leaving the city. I told her that it would be about 1600 as we planned to spend some time at the Hermitage during the afternoon. She politely, but sternly, informed me that we would be leaving *exactly* at 1600, not *about* that time.

"After parking across the street from the Hermitage, we met an American family we had met the previous day while renting the car. The gentleman had long hair and a beard and I felt he was probably a little on the liberal side. He noticed that I was wearing an American-flag tie tack on my lapel and remarked, 'You know, it would never occur to me to wear a pin like that in the United States, but I'd give my eye teeth to be wearing one now.' I asked if he thought some of his liberal friends should spend a few days in Russia, to which he replied,

'A few days, hell, just fifteen minutes. This has to be the biggest rip-off in the history of mankind.'

"Entering the Hermitage, we were like children in a candy store trying to decide what we wanted to see in the short time we had. The Hermitage is probably the most fabulous museum in the world and it has been estimated that if one spent just one minute, twenty-four hours a day, looking at each exhibit, it would take eleven years to see it all. We settled for the building housing the ancient Egyptian and Roman exhibits but couldn't begin to do it justice in two hours. I would recommend a visitor to St Petersburg, as it is now known, allocate at least three days to see this wonder of the world.

"Would you believe it? We left Leningrad precisely at 1600. What a coincidence!" With that, he laughed and then proceeded to say,

"At least we tried to leave at that time. Even armed with a map of the city, we got lost. Finally we found a street that looked vaguely familiar and found ourselves on the highway leading to the airport. There were no signs pointing to Moscow, but somehow we felt we were going in the right direction. When we came to a big circle with streets radiating in all directions, we went half way around and kept going in the same direction. Passing the airport turnoff we traveled several miles into the countryside. While the road surface was good, this just didn't seem like it should be the main highway to Moscow.

"Eventually we spotted a man and his wife walking down the highway in the opposite direction and remembering the admonishment I had received about *no detours*, I pulled over, stopped and yelled at the couple. The man came over, but he could speak no English so I said *Moskva* and he seemed to understand. He pointed back in the direction from which we had come then tapped on the back door window indicating he would like a ride. I motioned for him to get in and he seemed very grateful. Making a U turn, we headed back toward the city picking up his wife, who, by this time, had walked a quarter-mile down the road. I gave them cigarettes and they were all smiles.

"When we got back to the circle, he showed us where we had made our mistake. Had we gone three quarters of the way around the circle, we would have observed the big sign with arrows pointing toward Moscow and indicating it was Highway 10, After exchanging a couple of rounds of '*spasebas,*' we were on our way to Moscow at last.

"As we drove into the countryside, we noticed a striking resemblance to the Pacific Northwest. There were miles of lush green farmlands interlaced with rivers and streams. The villages were quite close together and we were amazed at the thousands of log cabins. Some of them must have been hundreds of years old, but it was impossible to tell as we saw new log cabins being constructed. None of the houses were painted except for the brightly colored gingerbread trim around the windows. Unlike our yards, there were no flowers and lawns. I do believe every square inch of yard space was devoted to the growing of vegetables. The only flowers were the geraniums growing in the window boxes.

"Because this highway was open to tourists and it being the main route between Leningrad and Moscow, we had expected it to be a show place of modern Russia. On the contrary, it was like suddenly turning back the clock about seventy-five years. Imagine all the people of a village drawing their water from one pump and women carrying it in buckets hanging from yokes. Many of the houses leaned like a coal chute and it seemed rather incongruous to observe so many of these ancient structures festooned with television antennae.

"This did, however, give us some clue as to how many families were occupying each house.

The surface of the two lane road was generally good and the main obstacles were such things as a woman with a herd of goats or the many horses and wagons. As for traffic, it was surprisingly heavy but consisted of about ninety percent trucks. Every few miles we observed

police checkpoint sta-
tions where we were
required to slow down
to forty kilometers per
hour. While the police
looked us over care-
fully, as we went by, we
were never stopped.
We couldn't help but
observe that after jot-
ting down something
on a note pad as we
passed—obviously our
license plate number—

Some farm homes weren't exactly level

the policeman cranked up a phone, apparently to report to the next
observation post. Now we understood why we were apparently not
followed. They didn't have to; they knew where we were at all times.
We also noticed that all closed trucks were inspected at each of these
checkpoints.

"When we arrived at the first of the three petrol stations that
showed on the map between Leningrad and Moscow, there was a
long line of trucks so I pulled in behind them. I had no way of knowing there were separate pumps for the cars and trucks in spite of the
fact they were both gasoline powered. A car pulled up alongside of
us and one of the two youths inside yelled and motioned for me to
back up. Not being able to communicate with him, I backed up. He
then swung in ahead of us, made a hard right turn over a concrete
island and made his way up along the right side of the line of trucks.
I figured he must know what he was doing so I followed suit.

"Sure enough, when I got up to him, he was filling his tank; I
chose another pump and put the hose into our gas tank. I pulled the

trigger on the nozzle but nothing happened. I walked over to the little building that housed the cashier and tried to ask her how to operate the pump. She indicated that I should be at another pump and I could tell she wanted money. I thrust two of my coupons through the window and headed back to the car. When I arrived back at the pump, I discovered that some joker had backed up to my pump sideways and had removed the hose from my gas tank. I jockeyed over to the pump the lady had directed me to and proceeded to pump my twenty liters of 'auto benzene' as the Russians call it.

"Meanwhile the two young fellows we had encountered earlier evidently spotted us as Americans and approached us speaking nearly perfect English. 'We would like to buy some American cigarettes,' one of them said. 'You know that is against the law and I cannot sell them to you,' I replied. 'However, I have some extra ones and I will give you a couple of packs.' They insisted they wanted to pay for them, but I refused. They were so appreciative they made me feel that if a couple of packs of cigarettes could make two friends for America, I should have brought a carload.

"One of the men pointed out that my left front tire was low. He pulled out a tire gauge, checked it, and then proceeded to his car where he removed a bicycle pump from his trunk. He must have pumped for ten minutes until he was satisfied the tire contained the correct pressure.

Russian fellows pumping up my tire

"Evidently they felt guilty about the cigarettes for they insisted on an even exchange. From their car they brought two small boxes of Cuban cigars. While the door of their vehicle was open, I heard the unmistakable voice of Frank Sinatra. I asked them what they had and they replied, 'it's a tape deck.' ' Do they sell Frank Sinatra tapes in the Soviet Union?' I asked. 'Heavens no,' said one. 'Then how did you get it?' I can still hear them say, as they drove away. 'Very difficult, very difficult.'"

With that, Hugh Williams announced that at this point he was going to leave the group in suspenders.

"That's a pun, son. Now a gentleman is here to join us as, we were promised by the Wheaties All-American pro-bowl athlete that gave us the treatise on jobs yesterday. I'd like to present Everett Sargent." Mr. Sargent made his way to the front of the room announcing,

"I'm not a public speaker, but I'll give it the old college try.

As for my college major," he continued matter-of-factly, "guess one would have to describe it as Heinz 57. I've taken so many courses in energy, all the way from fossil fuel to nuclear that I'm a modern version of that old moniker of 'Jack of all trades, but master of none,' That, plus what I've researched for this seminar, makes me feel at least a little qualified to contribute to this learning process. Indeed, it was when I started digging into related subjects that made me realize just how much more I have to learn.

"Mr. Williams, now fess up…You didn't tell this group that you had made several trips to Russia, did you? If you would be so kind as to tell us what you may have observed in that country on subsequent trips that may somehow relate to the subject of energy, I have a hunch that perhaps it will have a direct bearing on what's taken place in the last twenty years."

"Well, okay," responded Hugh, "but I feel as though I have been hogging the floor and that most folks were ready for a change of scenery now and then, up here in front.

Yes, I must confess I made at least seven or eight more trips to Russia, the first one after that 1972 trip occurring in 1991. Later in my 'Lowell Thomas' travelogue I'll be referring to a lovely Intourist Guide by the name of Tamara Donskiskh. She was one of the most gracious and knowledgeable ladies I have ever met in my life. All I can say is: somehow, I must have made a favorable impression on her and her friends in Novosibirsk. The powers that be in that Siberian metropolis called me in the middle of a night in September, 1991, asking if I had received their invitation. They asked me to return to Novosibirsk to teach capitalism upon the fall of communism. But I'm stealing my own thunder from future lectures, so suffice it to say I repeated a portion of my journey of 1972.

"On the Trans-Siberian train trip from Moscow to Novosibirsk, I couldn't help but observe hundreds and hundreds of tank cars almost completely covered with oil. The roadbed, in many places, wore a similar coating of that black substance. When I inquired about the situation, I was informed that it was not uncommon for workers to position a tank car under a spigot, turn it on and go for a long coffee break. Needless to say, the car would overflow and in some areas there were literally lakes of oil while, at the same time, folks in the next village would be freezing for they had no oil with which to heat their homes. Incidentally, those same conditions that existed in 1972 were still prevalent when I made my next trip to that area in 1991.

"As it was approaching an election year, upon my return home, I faxed this information to the three major candidates for president: President Bush, Governor Clinton and Ross Perot. I suggested how America might benefit from Russia's surplus oil problem, but again, to use an expression I used earlier, it was about as effective as peeing in the Pacific to raise the tide."

"Thanks, so much Mr. Williams," picked up Everett, "your experience certainly ties into what has transpired while you were 'away.' I don't know whether somebody read some of your frequent letters to the editors or dug up some archives and somehow retrieved your faxes. Perhaps it was just coincidence, but it apparently dawned on somebody that it didn't make sense for America to be so dependent on the OPEC nations and their fragile means of transportation, while Russia was drowning in oil. The president, having dissolved the Department of Energy, was forced to do what should have been done years ago in all phases of government, called in experts in many fields, including oil exploration, refining and transportation. Strange, but somehow folks in private industry can accomplish so much more than their so-called counterparts in government and they don't even have to appoint committees nor spend the public's money.

"When a report was rendered by the representatives of the oil industry, after a quickie trip to Russia, it more or less confirmed what you learned earlier, Mr. Williams. Upon learning that Siberia had more oil than Alaska and Saudi Arabia combined, the president dispatched negotiators to Moscow. They entered into an agreement with President Putin that called for America to send her best oil experts to Russia and provide all the equipment necessary to bring the Siberian oil fields up to speed. We sent experts in traffic and pipelines to teach the former communists the concept of supply and demand. Would you believe even some of the environmentalists went over also to help clean up the mess that had been left by seventy-five years of communists' 'good stewardship' of the land?

"And just what did we request in return? We signed an agreement to the effect that America had first call on any surplus oil that existed after all of Russia's needs were met. It was a win-win situation for both countries for Russia started catching up to the twenty-first century after their nearly seventy-five years of slavery and as their own demands for energy were increasing, there was no interruption of their exports to America for we developed new fields to keep pace. One of Russian's demands was that the United States extract more petroleum from our own Alaskan reserves for it didn't make sense for any country to exploit the natural resources of another while leaving their own untouched. No, we didn't ignore our friends in the Middle East but our new agreement certainly leveraged the price of oil down to a price we could live with. Now there is even talk of constructing a pipeline across that fifty four-mile stretch of the Bering Sea between Russia and Alaska. It would connect with the Alaska Pipeline and should an emergency arise, the petroleum could flow either way.

"It has often been said that sometimes we are so close to the forest we can't see the trees. Indeed, there were oil sources closer to home that had been ignored by the United States for many years. Southern Mexico, Central America and the northern portion of South America are sitting on some of the richest oil deposits in the world. Back in 2000, with the election of a new party and president in Mexico, the United States and its neighbor to the south agreed to an exchange. If Mexico would agree to the US building a pipeline to tap their oil fields in the south, America would agree to financing and constructing a freeway from the U.S. border for nearly the entire length of that country. I won't say we had an ulterior motive, but it does make it much easier to defend that pipeline should the need occur. Another benefit, aside from all the jobs the construction of that highway provided to Mexican workers, was the fact that many more Americans started vacationing 'south of the border' what with a beautiful highway liberally sprinkled with motels and RV parks along the right of way.

"I have much more to add along the lines of energy, but I'm afraid it's a little lengthy and your 'iron buns' are probably beginning to scream for a change of venue. Will you kindly let me continue this tomorrow?"

ROAD RAGE

As society searches for ways to control angry confrontations between motorists the U.S. Army has come up with a novel, but costly, solution—make sure their vehicles never make it onto the road. It all started when the Army wanted to upgrade its mobility with high-speed trailers and medium trucks to haul them. But because of poor contractor oversight, the first 6,700 trailers produced were mostly useless and downright dangerous—they actually damaged the vehicles towing them. The medium trucks designed to haul the trailers were in no better shape. Many cabs on the trucks were corroded upon delivery, and a drive shaft flaw has limited the 'safe' speed for these fast movers to a snails pace, 30 miles per hour. Did the Army take these contractors to task? Not exactly. The government didn't insist on a warranty for the trailers so it is out $51 million for the initial purchase and $4.3 million for the upgrades. Replacing the rusty cabs on the trucks will run up to $21 million, again, courtesy of the taxpayers. Before the government's General Accounting Office blew the whistle last fall, the Army was actually planning to order 18,000 additional trailers from the same contractor.

Capital Ideas
March/April 2000

CHAPTER 12

"I hope you're all taking notes," Mr. Williams announced the next day.

"Oh, didn't I tell you there *will* be a final exam at the end of this course?" While most of the 'class' laughed, some had an expression indicating they took Hugh seriously, at least for a moment until the laughter soothed their apprehension.

"Yesterday, I believe, I left us at—and I use the term loosely—a filling station, somewhere between Leningrad and Novgorod. We continued our journey toward Novgorod where we were to spend the night. Although it was only a little over four hundred miles from Leningrad to Moscow, they would not permit tourists to drive it all in one day. The scenery changed very little and one could not help but notice the oneness. When you've seen one Russian village, you've seen many for even the commissary buildings are nearly identical, much like chain stores in the states. As we proceeded south, even this relatively short distance, we noticed it was getting dark much earlier.

"Many cities in the Soviet Union have a *Kremlin,*—which means fortress—and Novgorod was no exception...

"Arriving at that city, we made a wrong turn but with the aid of a policeman, we had little difficulty in locating the Sadko Hotel. In fact, he stopped traffic from all directions to allow us to make a U turn in the middle of a busy intersection. People stood around and stared at our car and us as we parked in front of the hotel entrance. In the lobby, another group stared at us while I registered. Fortunately the girl behind the desk knew a

Kremlin of Novgorod

few words of English for the registration card was all in Russian.

"As it was nine in the evening, we assumed the restaurant was closed, in fact, we were directed to a buffet on one of the upper floors. After a very unappetizing snack, we went back down to the lobby only to hear music coming from a dining room. Upon entering, it looked like a nightclub packed to the rafters. People were eating and drinking while the dance floor was occupied by rock-and-roll dancers.

"Finding a table with two empty chairs, we proceeded to order a 'screwdriver.' What an experience! The waitress did not understand a single word. A family sitting at our table volunteered their services. We were surprised to hear them speak English as they claimed to be from Yugoslavia. Evidently their English was better than their Russian was for after a lengthy conversation with the waitress, that man said to me, 'she wants to know if you want some strawberries.' How they got strawberries from orange juice, I'll never know so we decided to settle for *wadka* and water. I should have remembered that in Russia, if you even mentioned water, you would receive mineral water. That is one time when the drink tasted much better than the chaser.

"I still had some Canadian Club in my room so decided to see if I could secure some ice. When the waitress came over, I grabbed my shoulders and shivered. I did better than the Yugoslavian had done for, lo and behold, she brought me a compote filled with ice. I should have taken a picture of it for we were to see very little more of this precious commodity in Russia. The weather was still so hot; the ice nearly melted before I could get it up to our room.

"Upon arrival on our floor, we secured our key from the chambermaid. In Russian hotels, one was required to leave one's key with the lady in charge of their floor each time they left. We heard stories to the effect that this practice enabled the secret police to go through one's personal belongings during one's absence, but we had no way of confirming this. We did recognize the word *Amerikanski* in her phone conversation, apparently to the doorman.

"Our room was considerably smaller than the one we had in Leningrad, but comfortable and clean. As in Leningrad, we had a pair of single beds radiating from a corner of the room with wooden sideboards. Just like everywhere else in the Soviet Union, the pipes in the bathroom were

View from our hotel window in Novgorod

all exposed. We thought it was for easier access but it seems they were one of the chief sources of heat piped from central steam plants. Though the bathtub was adequate, we never did quite figure out just how one was supposed to sit in one. As in Leningrad, the linen consisted of a long narrow strip of

material about the con-
sistency of cheesecloth,
which was supposed to
serve as a bath towel.

"The view from our
window the next morn-
ing was certainly a study
in contrasts as we gazed
down upon the many
log cabins interspersed
with new apartment
houses.

One of the 800 year old churches near Novgorod

"We went down to
breakfast, which was
identical to all we had eaten in Russia and the ones to be consumed
in the future. We decided to save our sightseeing coupon for an extra
tour in Moscow and 'go it alone' in Novgorod. Upon obtaining a map,
we found this was not too difficult as the historic points of interest
were displayed very prominently on that map in spite of the fact it
was printed in Russian.

"We had no problem driving out to the Monastery, which was several hundred years old and was being restored by the Soviet government. I did encounter difficulty, however, when I drove into a farmer's
yard in order to get closer to the 800-year-old churches. With dogs
barking, this man let me know, in no uncertain terms, that the sign
on the highway meant 'do not enter'. We proceeded back to the main
road, parked and then walked to the ancient churches.

"By the time we arrived back in Novgorod, it was 11:30 A.M. so we
decided it was time we resumed our trip to Moscow. After about an
hour's drive, we became hungry so we stopped at a village commissary
only to have the door slammed in our faces. I tried a trucker's stop but

somehow it didn't look too clean so I settled for a glass of '*lemonate*' as the Russians called any fruit drink.

"Another difficulty that we encountered in the Soviet Union was the practice of paying for our food in a cafeteria before making our selection. How could we know the cost of the food before going by the entrees?

"Stopping in more villages and again having more doors slammed in our faces, I decided to sneak up on the next commissary by parking around to the side. It worked as we gained entry before the proprietor realized we were foreigners. When we indicated we would like to purchase some oranges, we were greeted with the familiar *nyet*. Oranges were available only in the big cities and could cost as much as sixty cents each…a lot of money to a Russian, especially in those days.

"We decided to settle for some cookies and chocolate. We pointed to the cookies in the display case and the lady behind the counter pointed to the scales. I held up two fingers and it was at this time Winnie decided to try out our 'English-Russian dictionary. Using a phonetic pronunciation, she asked for some chocolate. Again, the scale routine and again, I held up two fingers. She took a piece of newspaper and wound it around her arm to form a cone, as they had no paper sacks in Russia. We could hear her dishing up something behind the counter but were unable to see just what it was. She folded over the top of the shaped container and indicated I must pay the cashier before she would give us our purchase. I recall that I thought that two rubles, thirty-eight kopecks was a little steep for cookies and candy but said nothing. I paid the cashier and took my receipt back to the other end of the store and carried out our goodies.

"As we started down the highway, Winnie asked me if I had ever heard of white chocolate, I had heard of it, but Russia was the last place I'd have expected to find such a luxury, Winnie tasted it only to discover we had purchased one hell of a lot of cube sugar. Upon checking our dictionary, we also discovered that the Russian word for confection and their word for sugar were very similar. It was about this time that it dawned on me when I had held up two fingers, we were talking about kilograms instead of pounds.

Propaganda sign along the highway

"This day was rather uneventful, as all the villages looked alike right down to the ever-present portraits of Lenin.

The weather was still beastly hot so the rainstorm we encountered was welcome. We had to stop while I attached the windshield wipers. For some reason, in Russia, at least on rental cars, the windshield wipers were kept in the glove compartment. When not in use, they were to be placed back in the glove box or the renter would be charged for them. Perhaps the citizens stole them, but for what reason was a mystery unless that was as much of an automobile any Russian could ever hope to own.

"With that, I'm going to relinquish the microphone to the gentleman that got me all pumped yesterday about energy. He promised to bring me up to date on a subject that was still but a dream in my day—superconductivity. Everett, if you please."

"Thank you Mr. Williams. Like a previous speaker, I'm not going to give myself the title of expert. I'm happy to share what I know about the subject with you but keep in mind, some of it is from memory and some is the result of research. I couldn't believe it when I checked the reference desk at the library, only to be told there are literally thousands and thousands of references to this subject. Mr. Williams, you probably recall that around the turn of the century, folks—even some scientists—jokingly cast off any research into superconductivity as a 'Flash Gordon in the pan.' Some, however, never gave up and you may recall the Japanese even powered a 150-ton ship with superconductivity as a source of power clear back in 1990. They had already had some success using this innovative force to run trains on dry land.

"After inauguration in 2009, the new president gave a speech wherein America was asked to work with the same resolve that Jack Kennedy demonstrated when he promised to put a man on the moon within a decade. America answered Kennedy's call and I'm sure, Hugh, you no doubt recall where you were on that memorable day in 1969 when the first man landed on the moon. As a student of history, I've often wondered why no correlation was made with the driving of the Golden Spike in Utah, exactly one hundred years earlier in 1869, completing America's first transcontinental railroad.

"The new president knew the benefits to be derived from the perfection of the theory of superconductivity. It could change living conditions for all mankind. With that, America embarked on a re-conversion spree not unlike that which she experienced at the end of World War II. Think tanks all across the country declared war on the high cost of energy and set their sights on perfecting superconductivity at room temperatures.

"You may recall that a couple of days or so ago, Mr. Paulson re-marked about not stepping on another speaker's toes and I have a hunch he was referring to the dovetailing of his subject of employment with my subject of energy.

"Perhaps I should also start back at the snow scene so you may get the drift. For over forty years now, scientists have been aware of the fact that about 85% of electric energy is lost through friction while being transmitted through conventional wires. Experiments using copper, zinc and aluminum proved that this friction could be eliminated, however, the phenomenon known as superconductivity could be achieved only at super cold temperatures about minus 470 F. From the brains of the Einsteins of the twenty-first Century came the solutions and a whole new world opened for those with imagination and the willingness to work.

"A previous speaker told us of the re-wiring of various cities in snow areas, hurricane prone areas and tornado alley. He didn't want to steal my thunder, so he graciously neglected to mention that the perfection of superconductivity led to the re-wiring of all of America.

"Perhaps we should now be holding a round-table discussion as you can readily see how energy is now interwoven with transportation and environmental concerns. Mr. Williams, you didn't include transportation on your wish list so, with your permission, I would like to elucidate a little on that subject. Obviously, with a drastic reduction in the cost of electricity, the electric cars, which had been nothing but a rich man's toy, became much more practical. The half-electric, half-internal combustion automobiles that appeared on the scene in your day are now more numerous than the polluting machines you were familiar with. The dramatic reduction in the cost of electricity was a real boon for the production of hydrogen fuel cells that now propel millions of vehicles.

"The Russians have made dramatic progress since their liberation from the yokes of communism. They always had been near the top in some technologies and have now come out with a new automobile called The Zaftra which they have merchandised as the car of tomorrow. It has all the bells and whistles and lives up to its name, which is Russian for 'tomorrow'.

"In addition to the fuel conserving features, the automobiles of today now offer life-saving devices as well. To augment the age-old back-up white taillights, a beeper sounds much like those employed on lift trucks. Also, the law requires that when one turns on windshield wipers, the lights be activated automatically and simultaneously.

"All cars today are equipped with an Onstar device that can bring help immediately anywhere without a word being uttered. A motorist merely needs to press a button, the equivalent of 911, and with GPS—Global Positioning Satellite—his position is immediately transmitted to summon help. Car-jackings are a thing of the past. Years ago, legislation was passed in many states that, in affect, outlawed the use of hand-held cell phones in autos. With the advent of voice recognition devices, car phones no longer are a safety factor.

"Highways today are much improved over what you were accustomed to at the turn of the century. In areas, which are subject to ice storms, the advent of economical electricity has inaugurated highways with heat. Special sensors are laminated into certain highway signs such as sharp curves, detours and the like so motorists are warned of such hazards long before they come into their headlights. They work on the same principle as your old fuzz-busters.

"All construction of new freeways in urban areas today is required to have median strips that will accommodate light rail mass transit systems. All new overpasses must be at least two feet higher than in your day, not only to allow for higher loads, but also to provide enough space for commuter trains and their overhead electrical apparatus,—pantographs. Nowadays, these overpasses have special drainpipes to supply runoff to the ivy planted at the base of each structure. The 'greenies' loved it as it at least gave the appearance that the whole country has not been cemented over.

"I don't know whether it was kissing up to the environmentalists to counter their constant bitching, but some communities started demanding that all new homes will be equipped with a cistern to trap rain water from roofs to be used for watering of lawns, washing cars, etc. wherever possible and practical. Some groups along our coasts want to copy Hong Kong's example of using two sets of plumbing wherever possible. Hong Kong is dependent on a pipeline from Mainland China for all their fresh water so they use sea water for flushing toilets and the water conservation in just hotels alone is tremendous…

"Another advent with the perfection of superconductivity is the widespread use of high-speed trains. This, in turn, brought about the increased use of super-hub centers by the airlines while reducing the traffic in our crowded skies. After all, it didn't make sense to fly between such cities of Portland, Oregon and Seattle, Washington when one could make this trip from downtown to downtown in less than an hour via surface transportation. Indeed, studies are now underway to establish super hubs such as the one being contemplated in the Tri-Cities of Washington and which, if completed, will serve Seattle, Portland and Spokane as each of these cities will be only about an hour away via the new super trains. This will allow for the supersonic jets to serve areas they had been barred from in the past. Some have even suggested a super airport on Long Island that could serve all the major population centers of the Northeast.

"Another by-product of this new technology was the environmental benefit. With the advent of electric cars coupled with the 85% increase in our electric supply without the addition of fossil fuel plants, the floundering Green Party was thinking about folding their tent. Oh, they're still hollering about the whales and really went ape when the powers that be finally discovered the best way to preserve the salmon runs in the Pacific Northwest was to bring sealskin coats back into style."

INFERNAL REVENUE

Some say it's just not fair for the National Taxpayers Union to pick on the IRS during tax season. Fine—we'll let the government itself do the talking instead. General Accounting Office auditors indicate that the tax agency is finally getting a handle on the basic business of accounting for incoming tax payments and outgoing revenues. But other parts of their recent report could have been lifted from the same documents they've been writing for close to a decade: "IRS continues to face the same pervasive systems and internal control weaknesses we have been reporting each year since 1992. One apparent "weakness" is a blind eye to criminals: the IRS mistakenly sent over a half million dollars in refund checks to a Baltimore tax preparer's address for years after he moved. Lucky check cashers in the neighborhood included a hair salon owner and a convicted drug dealer who was able to pay for a home-monitoring bracelet that was part of his sentence.

If this incident seems like a drop in the bucket, reach for your raincoat. Last year, the IRS found that 86 percent of the $1.25 billion in refunds made under the Earned Income Credit for low-income taxpayers were invalid. Do you think America's tax agency still deserves the moniker "Infernal Revenue Service"?

Capital Ideas
March/April 2000

Author's note: I'm still trying to figure out why we Americans are stupid enough to let our government take our hard earned dollars and give it to people who paid no taxes whatsoever then have the audacity to give it a nice sounding name such as Earned Income Tax Credit?

CHAPTER 13

"Now that I have *proved* that I am a 'jack of all trades and master of none,' I'm gonna' quit while the quitting is good. Also, I'm anxious to get back to the Russia of fifty years ago. Mr. Williams, do you remember leaving us in the rain on a Soviet highway about fifty years ago?"

"Indeed I do," replied historian Williams. "I can remember it like it was yesterday. I must say the Soviet Union was way ahead of the United States in the use of the then-new international-highway symbols. All along Highway 10, at least it was easy to ascertain how far it was to the next garage, petrol station or restaurant. We passed a couple of cafes that resembled our drive-ins, but each one was closed. In Russia they had no public rest areas and with such a shortage of service stations, as we knew them, the lack of restrooms can become a problem. Fortunately, there were lots of forested areas between Leningrad and Moscow and we made good use of them. Later we learned that others who had utilized these facilities were promptly arrested. Evidently the secret was not getting caught. It would have also helped had we recognized poison ivy.

"Glancing at my gauge as we passed another petrol station, I was sure that we had enough gas to make it to Moscow. How wrong can one be? The gauge suddenly began to drop surprisingly fast. Perhaps it was because the driving conditions along this road allowed us to travel at one hundred kilometers per hour.

"Soon a red light started flickering on my gas gauge. In Russia, this took place when the tank reaches the one-quarter mark. Soon the light came on steady and my wife started worrying. She had visions of me hitchhiking to get help and her waiting by herself. She then started praying and, shortly thereafter, a filling station came into sight. We were greatly relieved only to learn that the station was for trucks only. When I asked for auto-benzene, the attendant indicated it was another thirty kilometers down the highway. When Winnie asked me if I thought it did any good to pray in an atheistic country, I replied: 'Certainly, all the channels are open.'

"I would have made book that we could not make it, but by driving slower and with the aid of Winnie's prayers, we arrived at the outskirts of a rather large city. There was a city route and a by-pass route with a police checkpoint at the juncture. I pulled into the police station and asked 'auto-benzene'. The officer pointed to the by-pass route and sure enough, within about three miles, we limped into a petrol station...on the fumes.

"By this time, I had only one gas coupon good for ten liters left. I handed it through the window to the female attendant and she activated the pump with the same type of dial setup we had encountered earlier. I went back to the car and upon pulling the trigger on the nozzle, heard one quick slurp and zip, which convinced me that it would never get us to Moscow. I rushed back to the window, shoved two rubles through which purchased enough to almost fill my tank.

"At this time, it was getting well into evening and we were amazed to find it was starting to get dark so early in such a contrast to Leningrad. About twenty-five miles from Moscow, we came to a freeway. They called it a freeway, but the outside lane was reserved for trolley buses.

"Driving into Moscow was much like approaching New York. I must say we were quite impressed with the many high rises and an oh-so-scarce neon sign in a shop or hotel. Of course we had no idea where we were going. We knew only that we had been assigned to the Hotel Ukraina. I figured that all roads must lead to Red Square and this assumption proved to be correct in this case. We kept right on going through the heart of the city until we crossed the Moscow River. I felt we were getting away from the city center so stopped in a left turn lane. When the light changed, I just sat there ready to abandon the whole idea right then and there.

"With traffic behind me honking, a policeman soon rushed over to see what the problem was. He was quite irate until he discovered we were Americans at which time he couldn't have been nicer. He pointed back across the bridge then promptly positioned himself in the middle of the huge intersection, blew his whistle, held up his hands, stopping traffic from every direction to allow us to make a U-turn.

"Back downtown, near Red Square, we stopped at the Metropole Hotel. In the Intourist office, I found a lady that spoke a few words of English. She drew a crude map and indicated I should take Gorky Blvd. to Karl Marx, and then proceed along this street to Kalinin Prospekt, which would take us to our hotel. Following her instructions, we drove to the Hotel Ukraina as if we had done so a

Hotel Ukraina in Moscow

hundred times.

"The hotel turned out to be a huge structure about thirty stories high and, while built solid as a fortress, it looked much older than its twenty years.

"It seemed that Stalin had ordered several of these structures built and they were all identical. Some were apartment houses, one was the Foreign Trade Ministry and one housed the University of Moscow. It did no good to try to use the silhouette of our hotel against the sky-line for a landmark as we had only one chance in five of finding our directions in this manner. The natives casually referred to this type of architecture as Stalin Gothic.

"With that I'm going to take a coffee break myself," concluded 'tutor' Williams. "Now who is going to enlighten me while I enjoy that refreshment?"

OMINOUS BILL

It's a lesson Members of Congress never seem to learn, but one that Americans have been made painfully aware of for at least twenty years. When it comes to massive year-end spending bills entitled 'Omnibus Appropriations,' lawmakers have some ominous surprises in store for taxpayers.

The Fiscal Year 2000 Omnibus Reconciliation Bill has dealt America another royal flush, with wasteful what-nots like $500,000 for a 'pilot project on harmful algae bloom research' in South Carolina, $1.9 million for promotion of Southern Kentucky Tourism Development Association, $500,000 to help the city of Chicago develop technology based business growth, $975,000 for a Princeton, West Virginia hardwood center and $200,000 for the Long Island Bay Shore Aquarium. If you prefer marine animals to fish, you're in luck. The bill provides at least $5.65 million for harbor seals, Hawaiian monk seals and Stellar sea lions. Not to be left out, taxpayers will also shell out at least $585,000 for sea turtle research.

U.S. Senator and government waste-watcher, John McCain (R-AZ) estimates that the FY 2000 Omnibus bill is about twice as bloated at its 1998 predecessor, which contained some $7 billion in add-ons, earmarks and un-requested projects.

Capital Ideas
January/February 2000

CHAPTER 14

In response to Hugh Williams' invitation, a well-dressed older gentleman strode forward and introduced himself as Andy Solenski, the owner of the rest home. With Hugh Williams' corny sense of humor, he just had to ask him if he knew why so many Polish names ended in 'ski?' When Andy answered in the negative, Hugh jumped on it and informed him it was because none of them knew how to spell toboggan. This humor went over like a lead balloon but did receive one hell of a laugh...from Hugh Williams.

"Mr. Williams and members of the 'Conversation and Coffee Klatch,'" was the manner in which Mr. Solenski began his address. "I'm in the same boat as many of your teachers here to the extent I know a little bit about a lot of things and don't even possess a college degree. Guess you might say I graduated from the school of hard knocks. With your kind indulgence, I'd like to shed some light on one of my pet peeves, namely government waste.

"I know, you'd think after twenty years of bitching, we would have made a dent in this problem, but it keeps dividing and multiplying like a bureaucratic cancer. As I recall, back around the turn of the century, some of your chief complaints had to do with health care, immigration, the underground economy, ad infinitum. I don't know where to begin and I certainly don't want to invade another speaker's space, but as the previous speaker mentioned, perhaps we should be conducting this whole presentation in a round table forum.

"It was widely known that billions were being wasted just in health care and that's all I'll say in regard to that subject as that was one of the subjects you asked to be covered at the outset of these get-togethers. I happen to know that we have a beautiful lady that will address that matter in a future session. One of the areas where Uncle Sam is really taking it in the shorts is known as the 'underground economy.' Way back in 1990, it was estimated that the government was losing as much as $100 million annually through this method of conducting business. Let's face it, man instinctively is a trader and it's only human for us to want to trade, not just to circumvent taxes, but for convenience and the lack of paperwork. If an electrician or plumber wishes to trade his skills for dental work, who will ever know the difference? In some cases involving big-ticket items, once in a while a guy would get caught and the government would make an example of him, but it did little to slow down the 'under the table' transactions.

"Another big hemorrhaging that needed a tourniquet was the fact that over six million individuals and firms were filing no returns and paying no taxes. For years the IRS has been trying to improve its image and are easy to deal with if you're honest, but for the deadbeats, it became 'no more Mr. Nice Guy.' When the evaders are apprehended, they actually spend time in the slammer. They'll never catch them all, but they certainly have made a big dent. We are still experiencing a problem with the 'tax shelters' off shore. I won't say these are criminal, but when one considers there are about 480 banks in a very small town on a small island in the Caribbean, it makes one wonder.

"I believe another speaker alluded to the billions in loans given for college education that went unpaid. I can say there is very little outstanding since the feds finally decided to get serious about recovering these funds. It was very embarrassing for a doctor or lawyer to have his paycheck garnished, especially when they were just getting started in their careers. Needless to say, word spread fast and the loans were honored.

"For years, I have been complaining about this country's immigration laws. Our borders were as loose as a sieve and anyone could slip in virtually unnoticed. Every few years we would declare amnesty and we were stuck with a couple million more residents that couldn't even speak the language. Finally, some of the states started wising up. They declared English as the official language and refused to publish laws, ballots and other publications in other languages. Would you believe some states issued driver's licenses to folks who couldn't speak a word of English? When I inquired about this, I was told the tests were given in their language. I said fine, but the last time I looked, the road signs were still printed in English.

"As long as we're on the subject of immigration, what really galled me was our attitude toward so-called 'religiously persecuted' refugees. You may recall that around the turn of the century, hundreds of thousands of these folks descended upon our country. I know personally of many thousand Russians admitted under these programs. To add insult to injury, the churches would give them $150 to tide them over until they received their first welfare check. As far as I was concerned, Uncle Sam who kept hollering about the separation of church and state, was, in effect, recruiting for the churches favored by the Russians. What really took the cement bicycle was the fact that these 'refugees' received all of the best medical and dental care at absolutely no cost. In the State of Washington, they were even chauffeured to specialists in Seattle, for example, and the state supplied translators fluent in fourteen languages with access to those who interpret fourteen more languages. Way back in your days of 2000 they were paying these people $45 an hour.

"These benefits coupled with rent subsidies, food stamps, welfare, etc. made many of them better off than some of our older working Americans. It took a long time for the INS—Immigration and Naturalization Service—to wise up. It wasn't until the states started to complain that the records of these folks were examined and they discovered that in most cases, the immigrants had signed statements to the effect they were in good health. When some of these characters had their butts shipped back to their country of origin, word must have spread, as what had been whole colonies of hypochondriacs suddenly became very healthy.

"Another thing that stuck in my craw was the practice of certain liberal do-gooders who would visit the flop-houses and look under the bridges for the dregs of society. They would talk them into signing a statement to the effect they were chemically dependent and presto! They were suddenly entitled to $422 a month from SSI, in spite of the fact they never paid a dime in taxes in their entire life. Many were drifters and merely left their forwarding addresses at taverns and bars in various cities. In at least one case, by the time one guy's checks caught up with him, they amounted to over $20,000. That did it for me. A bunch of us got together and marched on the Federal Building protesting the fact that our taxes were being used to subsidize drunks and hop heads. Strange, but when these payments stopped, many of these 'victims of society' discovered they could work. No, we weren't so cruel as to let anyone freeze or starve. The government set up forest camps and these folks did have a choice as to whether they wanted a warm bed and hot food in exchange for building trails and clearing brush or whether they wanted to take their chances back under the bridges and in the flop-houses.

"As was pointed out earlier, billions have been saved by such programs as the consolidation of cities that shared a common border, the consolidation of counties and the vast reduction of postmasters, nationwide.

"I could probably go on for hours and I'm sure everyone here has his or her own horror stories when it comes to government waste. However, I'm going to quit with the understanding I may return if subsequent speakers don't completely cover my subject. Now, Mr. Williams, kindly let us know how you and your wife made out in Moscow."

"Thank goodness for my photographic memory. I believe I had just described the thirty-story building that was to be our headquarters for a few days before we boarded the train to Siberia. Shortly after checking into the hotel we encountered the same problems that had confronted us earlier concerning where we would be fed. Again, we found that the dining room had been reserved for tour groups and that we must eat in the buffet. In one of these buffets, we ran into an American couple we had met in Leningrad and enjoyed having a drink with them while comparing notes about the drive from that city. We told them of our near disaster with the empty gas tank and Winnie's prayers. During this conversation, we were pleased to learn that our meal coupons were good at all Intourist Hotels so we were not confined to just one venue.

"Bright and early the next morning, we were waiting for the restaurant to open only to find that it would not be ready for breakfast until eight o'clock. We sat in the park across the parking lot from the hotel, just watching the rush hour traffic when we decided to gamble on the buffet for a cup of coffee. It was even worse than what we had tried in Leningrad. Finally the restaurant opened and we were greeted with the customary eggs, burnt on the bottom and raw on the top. Only the marmalade made the black bread palatable.

"Walking across the lobby, we exchanged more dollars into rubles at the Soviet Bank. In those days, the ruble was artificially pegged at $1.34. Thus, when I cashed a twenty-dollar travelers check, I was given sixteen rubles and some-odd kopecks—incidentally, on one of my subsequent trips to Russia, in 1993 to be precise, I was able to purchase rubles on the street for a rate of about 7,000 rubles to the dollar. Talk about inflation! Next to the Soviet Bank was an adjoining Intourist office. I inquired about our train tickets for the Trans-Siberian but was informed that I would have to come back later in the day. I then asked for tickets to the circus and ballet and we were given our choice of nights.

"We decided to attend the circus that same night and the ballet the next night. When I questioned the Intourist clerk about transportation, I was informed that we could take a taxi to the circus, but as all taxis are assigned, it was not possible to secure one for the return trip and we would have to take Metro or a trolley.

"We spent much of the morning writing postcards and then decided to walk over to the American Embassy which was located just a few blocks away, across the Moscow River. It was an interesting walk but we could not overcome the feeling that we were in a glass cage as most of the citizens stared at us. We had been instructed to register at the embassy as soon as possible upon arrival in the Soviet Union and this was our first chance to do so. The American government liked to know where their citizens were. This was the only way they could help them should they have an emergency message for the tourist or if the tourists should disappear, they would have some idea of where to start looking for them.

"Upon entering the Embassy, we were very much surprised to see hundreds of copies of the Magazine *Amerika* displayed in the racks along the walls. It seems there was an agreement between the United States and Russia to the effect that we would distribute *Soviet Life* in America and they would do the same with *Amerika* in the Soviet Union. This particular issue had a picture of President and Mrs. Nixon on the cover. It showed them waving from the plane that had brought them to Moscow a little over a month earlier. Of course, the publication was printed in Russian, but the cover told us that it contained quite a lengthy article about the President's visit to Russia.

"When we asked what all those magazines were doing in the embassy, we were told that the Russians were not keeping their side of the bargain. I started to gather up an armload, announcing that I would distribute them. 'Oh no, you will be arrested and probably sent to prison,' was the response of the lady at the reception desk. We were advised that we could have a copy, but if we were caught selling it or giving it away, we might end up in jail. The lady even advised against leaving it anywhere that it could be traced to us. She said if I wanted to take a chance and leave it on the metro or a streetcar, that would be up to me. I didn't really believe her when she said the going black market rate for the magazine was five rubles when the price on the cover said fifty kopecks. The employees in the embassy were very envious of us when we told them of our planned itinerary as they were forbidden to travel more than fifty miles from the city of Moscow.

"We stayed around the embassy until the noon news came out. Every day they put out a mimeographed sheet with the latest news from the West. We then strolled back to our hotel, taking pictures as we went. Upon our arrival, we were nearly mobbed in the lobby, as the locals spotted the magazine sticking out of my pocket. They crowded around us and asked where we had purchased the publication and nearly cried when we informed them we had picked it up at the embassy. I wanted so much to share it with them, but looking at them it was impossible to tell just which one might have been our ticket to the Gulag.

"We had a good lunch, by their standards, and decided to take a drive downtown. Arriving at the Intourist Hotel near Red Square, we proceeded to the cocktail lounge. The weather was still unbearable and we were ready for a tall cool one. We were served by one of the most attractive women I had ever seen and she had a very good command of the English language. We ordered two screwdrivers and I gave her that bit about having a good looking nephew back home who was interested in obtaining some pen pals, especially the female variety. She wrote her name and address on a slip of paper and left it on the table. Later, when she returned with another round of drinks, she saw that paper and came unglued. She exclaimed, 'Hide that quickly: please don't let anyone see it.' The look on her face did more than anything to bring home the fact that we were truly in a police state. It was hard for an American to conceive that such conditions existed.

"We drove back to our own hotel for dinner where we knew that, as was the case in many large hotels, the menus were printed in several languages. One merely had to point to the entrée they wished.

"Having been discouraged about the availability, or the lack thereof, of taxis after the circus, we decided to take a chance and drive. We had been shown on a map where the circus was located and it looked like a cinch. Driving across the bridge, I saw where I wanted to go, but because of the no left turns, I wasn't getting there. I tried turning to the right, only to end right back to where I made the turn. After the second time, a cop whistled me down. He came over to the car, shouting, but again, when he discovered we were Americans, he couldn't be nicer. He showed me on the map where I had made my error and directed us to an underpass, which would get us to the other side of Kalinin Prospekt. I got lost two more times, but somehow ended up at the circus. The building that housed the circus was quite small with only one ring.

"We felt sorry for the orchestra performers, who were soaking wet from the unbearable heat. We were glad we had purchased a program, which we could use as a fan. I had to admit that the Russians really knew how to put on a show when it came to circuses. The performing bears and the trapeze acts would put most American circuses to shame. The clowns seemed to play a bigger role in Soviet circuses than they did in their American counterparts. Perhaps this was an attempt to induce laughter, which was very rare in the Soviet Union.

"Coincidentally, the people sitting right behind us were from Seattle and it was nice to be able to converse with someone other than Intourist help and ourselves. The couple seated on our right was on their way home from an assignment in the Far East where he had been working for the U.S. State Department. They were staying at the Hotel Rossiya, which was the world's largest with six thousand rooms. As it was not too far from Red Square where we planned to go, we offered them a ride. They probably had second thoughts about it later as I promptly got us lost twice en-route.

"After dropping them off at their hotel, we headed back to the Intourist Hotel where they had an express bar and restaurant. Seating ourselves in the lounge, we couldn't help but be impressed by the quality of the music. They had a seven-piece band dressed in Cossack uniforms. The big difference between them and an American group was the fact the amplifiers were on the balalaikas. Upon recognizing us as Americans, they promptly struck up 'Hello Dolly.' We even enjoyed a dance or two.

"The closest thing on the menu that even sounded like steak was beef tenderloin. We decided to take a chance and were pleasantly surprised to find it was much like our steaks back home, but it was cut differently. As was the case all over the Soviet Union, they did not have cuts of meat, as we knew them, but chunks as though they had been ripped and torn. These chunks of meat were cooked rare, as we liked them, and were very tasty. They even served dill pickles and potato chips on the side.

"We made our way back to our hotel. Even the nights were hot and the only breeze that was blowing was from the wrong side of the building. A shower helped, but air conditioning would have been more than welcome. Trying to dry with those Russian towels was something else. I later read a fitting description of that linen: like a dresser scarf.

"Because Winnie and I had been apart for two weeks, we still had a lot of catching up to do, but she picked a most inappropriate time to start telling me about a secret NATO submarine base somewhere in the Adriatic Sea. Evidently she had gleaned this information while visiting her daughter on the Island of Corfu. I waved my arms at her wildly while pointing to what was purported to be an AM radio on a small shelf on the wall. It had only three stations and when we tried to turn it off, we found that we could turn only the volume down, but it glowed all night. Something told me that it was listening to us more than the other way around. I truly think that was when the 'police state' moniker really hit home with her."

AIR FARCE ONE

The cost of presidential travel has been a hot button for years, but President Clinton's tab is likely to leave taxpayers tripping out. According to Congress' General Accounting Office (GAO), the bill for just three of Bill's 1998 travel forays into Africa, Chile and China topped $72 million—NOT including Secret Service costs, planning time for agencies and bureaucrats outside the White House and some military security personnel costs. Thanks to political stonewalling and jumbled expense data, GAO accountants could only focus on this snapshot of the chief executive's excursions. But at least $60.5 million of that total could be tracked down to the Defense Department's airlift budget which some members of Congress say is already starved for funds to meet troop deployment needs overseas. One reason for the hefty price tag was the number of vagabond VIPs Clinton took with him. On the African trip alone, the official government delegation topped 1,300 people.

During seven plus years in office President Clinton has traveled outside the U.S. for 186 days which likely brings the total cost for the government's top globetrotter near the $1 billion mark. In contrast, our last two-term president, Ronald Reagan, went abroad for 84 days during his tenure. All presidents have to travel, but has President Clinton crossed the line between travel and travail?

Capital Ideas
November/December 1999

CHAPTER 15

"I think this would be an excellent time to take a break as I'm sure you've had it up to here about Russia when it was the USSR. After our little seventh inning stretch, I'll introduce our next volunteer."

When the clatter of cups and the chatter died down, Hugh Williams called the gathering to order and announced, "We are indeed privileged today to pick the brain of a well-known surgeon, Dr. Dewey Jamieson. However, to give him a starting point, I'd like to relate what little I knew about the field of health care back in 2000.

"I recall that way back in 1992, I read a magazine article that really blew my mind. It pointed out that America was spending more per capita than any other nation on earth for health care, but had probably the least coverage. Why? To begin with, twenty- four percent of our health care dollars were going just to pay for the administration and paperwork. Was this ever corrected? Did we ever achieve uniformity of claim forms?

"Just to make the cheese more binding, another thirty percent of our health care costs went for what they referred to as 'defensive medicine.' That was the cost of the high premiums doctors had to pay for malpractice insurance. This all added up to fifty-four percent of every health insurance dollar and purchased no health care. Added to those facts, we were told that health care fraud was costing us an additional $200 billion annually. Indeed, enough money could have been saved to insure every man, woman and child in America with no hike in taxes.

"Many of us feared that the federal government would try to institute a form of universal health insurance. In fact one senator even remarked that such a program would have the heart of the IRS, the efficiency of the post office and the cost of the Pentagon.

"I always thought the very term health insurance was somewhat of a misnomer. No one can insure your health so we were paying premiums to guarantee the cash flow of your local hospital and the paycheck of your doctor. I knew of no other field where your customers took out insurance to see that you get paid. When one purchased so-called health care, they were also paying the insurance for the uninsured. The health care carrier was paying for the indigent and this was built into the cost of one's hospital room.

"All over America hospitals, especially in smaller communities, were strapped for funds because the occupancy rate was less than what was required to maintain a positive cash flow. At the same time, veterans were required to travel, sometimes hundreds of miles, to a VA hospital the government couldn't afford to maintain. I argued, to no avail, that it would have made a lot more sense to issue vouchers that would have enabled veterans to see their own doctor and be hospitalized in their home town. That would have helped the cash-short hospitals and offered better care to our veterans.

"With that bit of 'ancient history' I'll relinquish the microphone to Dr. Jamieson. The floor is yours, Doctor."

"Thanks Hugh. I feel honored to have been asked to address your 'college course' and hope that any staff members in attendance will feel free to butt in at any time should I overlook any pertinent points.

"Back in about 2000 while the country was enduring a recession, we were at least blessed with no inflation, except in the health care field. There was a great hue and cry from the public against the drastic increases in the cost of medical service.

"Somebody must have dug into the archives and retrieved the same information you referred to. I believe it was published in *Consumer Reports* in their July, 1991 issue. The first, and indeed the easiest, reform to institute was the establishment of uniform insurance claim forms. In fact, some computer manufacturers even included such blank forms in their original equipment software programs.

"It didn't take long for everybody and his dog to seize on what appeared to be an advertising coup. Some folks resented advertising on their software discs but it wasn't really different than paying for a movie and having to endure a lot of hype about other films, etc. The computer companies argued that the insurance forms were merely blanks, plus the pressure and allure of the big money spoke so loudly that the complaints couldn't be heard.

"I'd like to say this innovation lowered the cost of health care by the twenty-four percent alluded to earlier, but, while it made a dent, perhaps one of the biggest benefits was the decrease in the *rate* of insurance cost inflation.

"As for the high cost of 'defensive medicine,' this field yielded the greatest benefits by far for the general public. This was accomplished, not by the medical profession per se, but by the enactment of tort reform laws by the various states. Juries could no longer award hundreds of millions of dollars to malpractice plaintiffs, but were limited by projected earnings of the victims plus stipulated amounts for pain and suffering. In your day, Hugh, it was not unusual for doctors to pay insurance premiums well in excess of a hundred thousand dollars a year. Most of the savings, due to lower premiums, were passed on to the patients, especially by the smaller practices.

"About the time these reforms came about, the government also relaxed the rules governing Medicare allowing physicians to treat Medicare patients with elective services without penalty. Conversely, the government really cracked down on fraud and dealt harshly with anyone double billing, over-billing, charging for services not performed, unnecessary surgery and the like.

"As I mentioned earlier, there was a great demand for a house cleaning of government waste. Such groups as CAGW—Citizens Against Government Waste—added their weight to these demands and the powers that be soon yielded to the increased pressure.

"I hope I'm not stealing anybody else's thunder when I comment on waste, but much of the cost of health care could be attributed to this aspect. When the general public discovered how much they were paying for health care for immigrants, especially illegal ones, they were really ticked.

"For example, as you alluded to earlier Hugh, in your state of Washington, back in twenty-aught two, the state paid interpreting companies to provide immigrants with translation services at various medical facilities and in twenty-eight languages.

"This was necessitated by the fact that America had still not determined that her official language was English but that's a whole different subject that will no doubt be addressed by someone more versed on that subject than I am. America was being literally flooded with so-called refugees, and, as such, they enjoyed better health care than millions of retired and low-income working Americans that had been paying taxes for their entire working lives. The state of Washington gave those 'refugees' the best of medical and dental care and even furnished cars with drivers to escort many of them to major health centers such as those in Seattle, for highly specialized cancer treatments and the like. It was rumored that those 'refugees' received not only dental care, they received gold fillings. Indeed, they received crowns, which in your day, Mr. Williams, carried a price tag of about $750 each.

"As you may recall, Hugh, in your stomping grounds of Clark County, there were thousands of Russian immigrants. Most of these folks claimed they were victims of religious persecution, which automatically qualified them as 'refugees.' They were brought in by the various churches and given $150 to tide them over 'til they received their first welfare check and they immediately became wards of the state.

"I don't like to get too political, but these folks soon learned how to milk the system and contributed greatly to the cost of health care. If such practices were so prevalent in Clark County, Washington, imagine what it must have been on a national scale?

"If an individual wished to sponsor a foreigner, even for a short visit, he or she had to sign an affidavit to the effect they would be responsible for all their guest's needs while on U.S. territory. When Uncle Sam finally wised up and imposed the same restrictions on the alleged 'refugees' certain churches in this country no longer had the American government filling their pews for them. Could that have been perceived as a violation of separation of church and state?

"A closer examination of the immigrant problems revealed that we were admitting folks with every known disease including AIDS and even folks in wheel chairs. Now, anyone wishing to emigrate to the U.S. must pass a rigorous physical examination or have a host willing to accept the burden of providing care for them.

"Perhaps one of the biggest examples of waste in the medical field was the federal government. Horror stories started leaking out about the policies in effect in Veteran's hospitals all over the country. Supplies were dumped so they could be replenished just to keep from losing appropriations for the next year. Would you believe when patients in government hospitals were taken to the door in a wheel chair to be discharged, the wheel chairs went with them? When questioned about this practice, the investigators were informed there were no inventory records kept for such equipment. Needless to say, after a thorough investigation, federal hospitals began functioning with a much leaner budget."

"With that, Hugh, I'll relinquish the podium as I'm sure our audience is ready for more of the Soviet Union, circa 1972."

CHAPTER 16

"Thanks, Dr. Jamieson, I became so engrossed in what you were relating, I forgot where I left off in Russia. As I recall, I believe we had attended the Moscow Circus and had retired after taking welcome showers.

"Bright and early the next morning we were in the dining room having breakfast when we encountered the couple we had met at the car rental agency in Leningrad. When we asked them how they enjoyed the drive to Moscow, they replied, 'terrible.' It seems they had taken the wrong road out of Leningrad, just as we had, but they made the mistake of trying to pass the second police checkpoint station. It didn't take long for them to get hauled to the local lock-up and, if I could believe him, he claimed he had to write 'I'll never take the wrong road again' fifty times. They said they were having a miserable time; they couldn't get tickets to the circus or ballet, and to top it off, the daughter had contracted pneumonia. They had very little good to say about Russia and couldn't wait to get out.

"Back at Intourist, I was still getting the run-around about our rail tickets. I was getting a little concerned and wondered if word had finally filtered down about the restrictions against individual Americans traveling east of the Volga. We had signed up for a three-hour bus tour and were surprised to find only seven other people on our bus. They segregated tourists by their respective languages, thus eliminating the necessity of having to repeat their spiels in several tongues.

"It was a very interesting and informative tour, which was well sprinkled with history, but surprisingly enough, very little propaganda. Much to our surprise, they took us down back streets to show us log cabins in the heart of Moscow; all were still used as residences.

"Back at the hotel, after lunch, I again checked at Intourist, only to be told to come back tomorrow. I then inquired about the possibility of hiring an interpreter, as I wanted to make a sales call on the head of the Soviet Steamship industry, known as Morflot. The lady said, 'that will be nine dollars and eighty cents, American.' I replied, 'How do you know the price when you don't know how long I will need the translator?' 'Makes no difference, fifteen minutes or three hours, price same.' She also informed me that I would have to tell her every word I would be saying to this man and that I would say these words and these words only. I said, 'how do I know what I will say until I hear his response? If he greets me with a polite hello, I'll respond accordingly, but if he is abusive, I might tell him where to put his steamship line...but that would be a physical impossibility.' She repeated, 'You will tell me every word, and these words you will say only and nothing more.' I told her to forget it, that I couldn't make a sales call under those circumstances and I walked out of her office.

"Driving in Moscow had proved to be so nerve racking that we decided to turn in our car a couple of days early. We drove down to Red Square to the Hotel Metropole where we were to surrender the vehicle. The first thing the clerk did was to look for the windshield swipes. Coincidentally, we had driven exactly one thousand kilometers. They explained we were entitled to a refund and issued a *spravka* or certificate but they also explained we would not get it until we returned to the States. I pocketed the *spravka* with a snicker as I had been told by many people that Intourist does not give refunds. Even my travel agent was very surprised when I later received a check for about $22.00.

"Walking through the tunnel under the huge intersection in front of the hotel, we were surprised to see hawkers selling lottery tickets. There was quite a maze of tunnels in

Winnie near Lenin's tomb in Red Square

that area and they were crowded with people rushing to and from the subways. The people seemed to be well dressed in contrast to what we had always heard. The women wore brightly colored dresses and many ladies had dyed hair, eye shadow and lipstick. You couldn't imagine so many shades of red hair. 'We walked across Red Square to Lenin's tomb.

Author dressed conservatively in Red Square

"They had a changing of the guard every hour with men in sharp uniforms goose-stepping across the cobblestones. We took pictures and were surprised to see the Russians taking pictures of us. Perhaps it was because I was wearing bright red double-knits and my loudest Hawaiian shirt.

"Children were coming up to us and saying 'chewing gum,' a commodity which was not available in the Soviet Union. When I asked a tour guide; 'how do they know we are Americans?' she responded, 'you've got to be kidding.'

"Walking back across the square, we decided to tour Gum Department Store, which was the largest in Russia. It was a massive layout with covered malls and many separate alcoves that had been individual shops before the Revolution. We looked at clothing on display and the prices were very high, even by our standards, while the quality was very poor. There were lines of people at the shoe departments, but the most popular items seemed to be the yard goods. I stuck my head into a grocery section, but my wife couldn't stand the smell. You wouldn't believe the meat department. I never saw a piece of meat that I could recognize, just chunks of fat with hairline strips of lean running through them. The poultry in the case was complete with feathers.

"Leaving Gum Department Store, we made our way to one of the entrances to the Kremlin as the ballet was to be presented in the Soviet Hall of Congress.

Soviet Hall of Congress in The Kremlin

"We were delighted to find such a modern structure, complete with escalators and air-conditioning. That building was a sight to behold, with ornate lighting, gold ceiling and much red velvet trim. The balcony had arms along each side of the auditorium sloping down to the main floor level.

"We were seated in what I considered two of the best seats in the house and, although we were not ballet fans, we welcomed the air-conditioning. The Russians prided themselves on punctuality and, precisely at seven o'clock, the house lights dimmed and the orchestra started playing.

Bolshoi Ballet Theatre

Much to our surprise, however, the curtain remained closed until about eight minutes after seven. Suddenly the house lights were turned up full strength and the orchestra struck up the Soviet National Anthem. Of course everyone stood but they suddenly started applauding and looking our way but just above our heads. We looked up to our right and couldn't believe our eyes. There in the State Box stood Mr. Podgorny and Mr. Kosigyn. I would love to have snapped a picture, but the expressions on the faces of the guards just a few feet from us, told me otherwise. They were very tough-looking men and I have a hunch they knew where every foreigner was sitting that night. In Russia, once a ballet or opera started, no one was allowed to enter or leave the auditorium until intermission.

"Surprisingly enough, we actually enjoyed the ballet. We were told it was called Sleeping Beauty and the acting, dancing, costumes, sets and lighting were something we would never forget. It certainly lived up to its name of *Bolshoi*.

The only sour note was the odor of some of the audience. When one left, upon their return, one didn't have to imagine where they'd been. Public sanitation by American standards didn't exist in the Soviet Union.

"At the conclusion of the performance, we walked back to the Intourist Hotel as we were quite hungry and our mouths watered for another one of those steaks. The meal was as good as the one we had the previous evening and the orchestra was just as enjoyable.

"I did not want to go through the hassle and red tape of being assigned a taxi so we went outside where many of them were scurrying by. I tried in vain to hail one but they paid no attention although many were empty. Feeling that everyone is a capitalist at heart, I decided to try a new approach. I held up two fingers and yelled, '*dvah rubles*'—two—and sure enough a driver screeched his brakes and in Russian asked, 'where to?' I replied, 'Hotel Ukrainia,' and he motioned for us to get in. Obviously he was not supposed to pick up an extra fare and he probably had to account for his time, for when I looked at the speedometer, it read one hundred forty kilometers per hour. This was through the main streets of Moscow, and Winnie buried her head in her hands, as she couldn't stand to look.

"When we were finally stopped by a red light, another taxi pulled up alongside and a conversation ensued between the two drivers. I said to Winnie, 'Don't look now, but I think they are going to drag.' Sure enough, we hit just the high spots crossing the bridge over the Moscow River. I don't know how he made it into our hotel parking lot, but with a little fish-tailing, he pulled up to the door.

"He pulled the flag down on the meter and said in broken English, 'no meter, no pay...souvenir.' I reached for my cigarettes and he said, '*nyet*, no smoke, please, souvenir.' As he had looked all around before the start of the conversation, I felt he was not a member of the secret police so I decided to take a chance. I reached into my wallet and gave him two American dollar bills which brought tears of joy to his eyes.

We had heard about how anxious the Russians were to get their hands on American money, but this was the first proof that we had encountered. Evidently, they wanted western currency to purchase goods at the stores that accept western currency only. We soon discovered that most of the merchandise in those *Berioska* stores, as they were called, was either not available to the average Russian or the prices charged in the regular stores were exorbitant.

"This seems like an appropriate place to leave you until tomorrow, same time, same place."

CHAPTER 17

"Good grief. I thought the novelty would have worn off by this time," were the remarks the next day's audience was greeted with. During a conversation with Dr. Laurel, the good doctor volunteered that many of the folks on the staff were like most other people. They knew a little bit about a lot of things but not a lot about a given subject. Hugh asked the doctor for a 'for instance' to which the doctor replied,

"You remember, Hugh, that a lot has been said about 9/11 and the effect it had on America. Well, I'm here to tell you that many businesses as well as individuals used that terrorist attack for an excuse to do things they might not have done otherwise. For example, the sudden drop in airline travel gave some of the airlines a reason to hit on Uncle Sam for subsidies. Many companies would have loved to use 9/11 as an excuse to raise prices, but the Clinton recession precluded them from doing so.

"Not all of the fallout from the first attack was bad, however, as it eventually gave President Bush justification for renouncing the Panama Canal Treaty wherein Jimmy Carter gave away one of America's most valued possessions. That whole sad episode was a case of industrial-strength stupidity besides being illegal as hell.

"No, President Bush didn't take back the canal, per se, but he did announce to the world, and in no uncertain terms, that America was ready, willing and able to defend it against all enemies both foreign and domestic. This is an example, Hugh, of a subject that you would no doubt enjoy hearing about, but it doesn't justify taking up the time of all our participants for a whole session a-a-n-n-d, are you ready for this? Would you believe that Carter was awarded the Nobel Peace Prize?"

When Hugh's blood pressure started dropping from the 200 over 100 that this remark prompted, he could only answer with:

"You've gotta' be kidding. Thanks, Dr. Laurel. What perfect timing. I was about to suggest that perhaps we had reached the point where we *should* change the format of our meetings to round table discussions."

Word quickly spread throughout the resort complex that 'Professor' Williams' coffee klatches were to become really interactive. All members of the audience were encouraged to contribute pertinent information concerning any and all significant events that occurred during the last twenty years.

When the next exchange was called to order, Hugh Williams was both surprised and gratified to see a virtual sea of upraised arms when he asked for volunteers.

"I've always been deathly afraid of public speaking," said a timid soul in the very back row, who identified himself as Bat Roberts, the younger brother of one of the resort residents. "But for what it's worth, I would like to put in my two cents worth.

"I don't know if you were a sports fan but there's been a dramatic change in the manner in which the International Olympics are conducted. The cost of hosting those games became prohibitive to the point where only a handful of cities could raise the funds necessary to lure those events. Somebody came up with the bright idea of dividing both the winter and summer events into quarters, thus making it possible for even relatively small venues to sponsor a much smaller program with only twenty-five percent of the athletes over a three- or four day time span. You may be surprised to learn that a city as small as Bend, Oregon hosted a scaled-down portion of the Winter Olympics in 2018."

"An excellent example," Hugh responded, "of what I had in mind when I announced a change of format for our daily get- togethers."

"With that," continued Professor Williams, "we take you back to the Soviet Union of fifty years ago and like an old old TV show, '*You are There.*' "After a good night's sleep, we arose early as we had booked a tour of the Kremlin. Immediately after breakfast I again went to the Intourist office, as by then, I had become quite apprehensive about our rail tickets. When I approached the same lady I had been dealing with, I was confronted with: 'Give me thirty-eight dollars, American.' Naturally, I asked why and she replied,

'You have been reassigned.' "My heart sank as I figured they had made other arrangements for us and I would not get the railroad trip I had dreamed of all my life. I gave her two twenty-dollar travel-

Winnie with Kremlin across the river

ers checks and she gave me less than two dollars change. I asked about the discrepancy and she advised that she had to deduct some for commission for cashing the checks. I jokingly said, 'You filthy capitalist.'

"She explained that instead of two berths in a four-berth compartment, we had been

Churches within the Kremlin walls

reassigned to a private compartment of our own. She then handed me our railroad tickets and instructed us to be at her office at nine the next morning.

"We boarded the bus that was to take us to the Kremlin, and we were disappointed to learn it was a walking tour.

"It would have been quite pleasant had it not been for the extreme heat. The Kremlin was filled with history and our guide was well versed on her subject. We toured the cathedrals within the Kremlin walls, of which there were three, and stood in wonder at the icons and fabulous wealth these buildings contained. At one time, there had been twenty-eight churches in the Kremlin, but the communists had destroyed twenty-five of them.

"At the conclusion of that expertly guided tour, we spent some time at the Lenin Armory Museum. A person should devote a whole day for that alone as the contents are fantastic. It contained everything from the gowns worn by Katherine the Great to the carriages that carried

142

St. Basil's Cathedral at end of Red Square

the czars and visiting royalty between Moscow and the Summer Palace in Leningrad. We enjoyed viewing the many newly-weds there that felt such a visit blessed their marriage.

"In spite of the cobblestones, we enjoyed a walk all the way across Red Square to St Basil's Cathedral which anchors one end of the square not far from the 'Hall of Persecution'.

"We had previously been shown the KGB Headquarters, which was described at the tallest building in Moscow. As I gazed at the eight-story structure, I remarked, 'no way.' 'On the contrary,' our guide responded, 'you can see Siberia from there.'

"Back at the hotel, Winnie decided she wanted to start packing, write some postcards and rest before the start of the next day's long journey. We had heard that conditions on the Trans-Siberian Railroad were quite primitive and she wanted to be prepared.

"I had made up my mind that I was going to get some new batteries for my tape recorder as mine were completely dead. One night when we had returned to our hotel, we found my tape recorder had been set on 'play' and my new batteries were dead. We would never know how this had happened and could only speculate.

"I suggested to Winnie that I make a big sign with a phrase that meant, in effect, 'fornicate communism' and place it in one of our suitcases, but she quickly vetoed the idea. My response was that if it caused a stink, they would have to admit they were going through our baggage. I lost the argument and perhaps that's why I'm here today to talk about it.

"I went back to the lady at Intourist that had been so helpful and whom by this time had become quite friendly. I explained that I wanted to purchase some batteries and showed her the size I wanted. She instructed me to catch a cab and go to the Jupiter Shop on Kalinin Prospekt. I thanked her and went back to the lobby to be assigned a taxi. When I secured one, I told him, 'Jupiter,' but they pronounced it Yoopiter. I know I said it just as the lady had but he just didn't understand. I rushed back into her office and she wrote a note in Russian which I showed to the driver and he said, 'oh yoopiter,' exactly as I had pronounced it.

"It was not too far to the shop where the driver indicated he would wait. Upon entering, I was surprised so see such an assortment of cameras, radios and tape recorders. I showed the batteries to a clerk and was directed to the other side of the store. After being directed and redirected several times, I came to the conclusion they had no batteries in spite of the fact they were required to operate many of the units they offered for sale. Each clerk kept repeating 'electra, electra.'

"I decided that while at that camera store, I would attempt to purchase some colored slides. I knew the meter was running on the taxi, but decided to take a chance. I said 'slides' and the clerk responded with 'slides' and showed me a beautiful selection. There were about ten strips of five each and I told him I wanted all of them. He didn't understand so I added up the total number of kopecks required for all of them and went to the cashier and presented that amount. When I returned with my receipt, he got the message and handed me one of each. One could lose a lot of time trying to shop in Russia, as every clerk, even the waitresses, carried an abacus, however, some of them could no doubt figure faster in their heads. Some could add large sums on that device faster than I could on an adding machine.

"Returning to the taxi, I said 'electra, electra' and the driver got out and motioned for me to follow him. We walked down to the next block and he asked the clerk, in what appeared to be a hardware store, about batteries. When he received a *nyet*, we headed back to the taxi. He drove me all over Moscow, picking up a couple of his friends on the way. They talked a mile a minute, but, of course, I couldn't understand a word. We finally arrived at a store, miles and miles away from my hotel and, again, received the familiar *nyet*. We then raced down the street on a dead run to another store and, at last, hit pay dirt. They had batteries that fit my recorder but I was skeptical as they appeared to be wrapped in paper instead of the aluminum I was accustomed to. They were only thirteen kopecks apiece so I thought I would gamble on them. I felt it was a cinch I would not be able to secure any in Siberia.

"The driver walked with me back to the taxi and indicated for me to wait while he disappeared up the street. Shortly, he returned with his two friends and there was more jabber all the way back to where he had picked them up originally. I did not see any money change hands, so could only assume I was paying for their ride.

"I arrived back at the hotel just in time as the weather really cut loose. The wind was blowing down traffic signs and breaking windows accompanied by torrents of rain. I entered the lobby just as it hit. Winnie was getting quite concerned about me, especially when she heard the sound of breaking glass. I had been gone over three hours and she was sure I had been picked up by the police. All through the Soviet Union she was so afraid my big mouth would get us into trouble and all the while *she* was the one who was more critical.

"We had planned to take a boat ride to Gorky Park and then to downtown, but the sudden change in the weather altered our plans. I had called the American couple, whom we had met in Leningrad and again in Moscow, and arranged to meet them at the Intourist Hotel later in the evening. Making a telephone call in Russia was quite an experience with no telephone directories and with each hotel room assigned its own direct number.

"Speaking of phones, ours rang several times and each time it was some guy sputtering a lot of Russian. I politely said I didn't understand but he kept calling back. I finally said, '*Russkiy nyet*, English *da.*' He finally gave up. I couldn't help but get the feeling he was a plant trying to determine if we comprehended Russian.

"I still wanted to see Gorky Park so we went back to my friend at Intourist. She wrote a note for me explaining we wanted a ride to the park and asking the driver to wait a few minutes while we made a hurry-up tour. We did not have the time to try the capitalism bit on a cab driver again so we went back to the lobby to be assigned a taxi.

"Immediately upon entering the cab, the driver offered to give me twenty rubles for ten American dollars. I said, '*nyet.*' Then he offered forty rubles for only twenty dollars. Receiving the same negative answer, he upped the ante to one hundred rubles for forty dollars. I again replied in the negative and he offered two hundred rubles for fifty dollars. I somehow pegged this man to be a member of the secret police. I replied, '*Nyet*, I do not wish to visit your salt mines.' He evidently got the message for he quickly dropped the subject.

"He took us to Gorky Park and waited while we literally ran through the amusement area. I had especially wanted to see the huge Ferris wheel, which I had heard about, and regretted I did not have time to ride it. They had many rides that looked as though they had been imported from America, such as the Mad Mouse.

"The driver then took us to the Intourist Hotel where we met our American friends. They were not feeling too well so they had only a couple of drinks while we enjoyed another steak. Seated at our table was a computer salesman from Denmark who spoke excellent English. He called our attention to three girls who were standing in the doorway and explained they were ladies of the evening, 'night butterflies' as they called them, and wanted us to invite them to our table. He warned us that one of them would no doubt report everything that took place.

"As we wanted to learn everything we could about Soviet culture, we invited them to join us. Two of the girls were very friendly but, sure enough, one of them never even cracked a smile. She acted as though she didn't understand what was being said, but somehow I got the feeling she never missed a word. When the women discovered they were going to get nothing but conversation, they left us after one drink. Our Danish friend had been correct and we began to suspect that he didn't spend all his time selling computers.

"With that, I'm forced to call it a day, but tomorrow I promise to start relating our adventures on the Trans-Siberian Railroad.

"You may have noticed that I have skipped the daily vignettes but keep in mind, they seem like they occurred only yesterday and if my loving daughter could save them from the dust heap for over twenty years, I feel I should share them with you. Now, don't you all cheer when I inform you that this will be the last one."

COP-OUT

Go directly to jail, do not pass 'go', do not collect $8.8 billion. That's what some would like to do to the federal government's high-rolling monopoly game being played with local police departments.

Although the Clinton Administration likes to brag about its program to add 100,000 more police to the streets by the end of the year, other numbers tell a different story. Crime rates have been dropping since 1991, long before the White House got into the act. Worse, many of the positions supposedly created by the $8.8 billion initiative, are fictitious. Although Nassau County, New York got $26 million to add 383 police to its rolls, by the middle of last year, officers there had dropped by 218. The Administration claimed that Spokane, Washington added more than ninety cops to the beat because of federal money, but the real number was closer to two dozen.

Alexandria, Virginia could not produce documentation that the $440,000 grant it used to buy equipment actually beefed up the size of the force. Waste watchers, in and out of government, found at least 100 communities with irregularities like these. Now, the White House wants $6.4 billion more apparently to repeat past mistakes with additional so-called 'Cops on the beat.'

Capital Ideas
May/June 1999

CHAPTER 18

The next day was such a beautiful Indian summer day that Hugh Williams had doubts about the size of the attendance he might expect at his seminar. His concerns were unfounded as since he had started asking for attendance records, his estimate of an even larger crowd than usual was borne out by the number of sign-ins.

"Next?" Hugh asked into the mike. The first hand to shoot up belonged to Lester Jeffries who identified himself as president and CEO of the holding company that operated rest homes nationwide.

"In my profession, like it or not, I am forced to do my share of public speaking and I'd like to express my opinion regarding tort reform and frivolous law suits. I don't know how many of our guests are aware that a large chunk of their monthly rental at our establishment goes straight to our insurance carriers to pay the sinfully high premiums for our liability coverage. Indeed, we've had patients die from nothing more than old age, yet we are sued for negligence. If ever a relative could prove that their loved one was not getting the best TLC possible anywhere, perhaps higher compensation may be justified. However, this retirement resort should not be penalized for the sins of other institutions.

"Some of the guests may recall that a couple of months ago they received slight reductions in their monthly statements due to the successful lobbying at both the state and federal levels and the legislation that resulted from that effort.

"Some states went so far as to penalize those that filed frivolous law suits. The attorneys had a cow but the judges welcomed it as it reduced their dockets significantly. In some states the law provides that should a suit be deemed frivolous by a jury of the plaintiff's peers, the plaintiff will have to forfeit the amount sought plus attorney's fees. Indeed, some have followed Britain's lead and also tacked on all the court costs, including those of the jury. Think about it, would any of you pursue this line of recourse unless you were sure your case was a slam dunk?"

"Thank you very much Mr. Jeffries. You certainly hit upon a subject that is no doubt dear to the hearts of many of my fellow guests. You remind me of some of the lawsuits I recall happening not too long before my accident. I would not be too surprised to learn that even today folks are still talking about such cases as the one wherein an elderly lady put a cup of coffee between her legs while driving away from a drive-up window and when she burned her privates, she sued McDonalds for an astronomical sum.

"I also seem to remember a fellow who purchased a motor home and, while driving down the highway, put it into cruise control and proceeded to the galley to prepare a sandwich. Needless to say he totaled the vehicle. He sued Winnebago Corporation and collected over a million dollars plus a new RV. I understand that Winnebago now puts warnings on their vehicles to advise others against the stupidity practiced by the idiot who thought those units drove themselves.

"I really think the one that takes the cement bicycle is the case where a man smelled so bad, officials finally had to insist that he not visit the library. He took them to court and was awarded a fantastic sum as the court ruled that it was his constitutional right to stink.

"Now, I suppose many of you are ready to step back again in time to Communist Russia, circa 1972. As I promised, we were now about to board the Trans-Siberian Railway train that was to take us about 6,000 miles across the steppes of Russia.

"Sunday, July 9, dawned hot and humid, as had every day we had been in the Soviet Union. That was to be my big day as we were to board the Trans-Siberian Railroad train to journey all the way across Russia to the Sea of Japan. We had seen the best of Leningrad and Moscow and I had thoroughly enjoyed the auto trip between those two cities. However, by now, my wife and I had become weary of crowds and eagerly anticipated the privacy of a train compartment and the prospect of cooler weather in Siberia.

"We arose early, packed our bags and by eight o'clock were waiting for the restaurant of the Hotel Ukraina to open for breakfast. We had been instructed to report to the Intourist office by nine that morning and this was one appointment I didn't want to miss.

"We were assigned a car with driver who loaded our luggage and whisked us off to a huge railway station. Upon arrival, he whistled for a

Railway car that took us to Novosibirsk

porter to help us with our baggage. That man must have been practicing for the Olympics, for we were hard pressed to keep up with him as we made our way through the crowds to the platform where our train was waiting. He took our suitcases into our compartment but, as so often had been the case, he refused to accept a tip.

"We were pleasantly surprised to find the compartment was almost identical to what one might expect to find on American trains during World War II.

'It had ample room, an upper and lower berth, a table complete with tablecloth and what might be described as an easy chair.

Winnie in our train compartment

"There was lots of storage space over the corridor and above the two doors, one of which led to a room containing a sink that was shared with an adjoining compartment.

"The train was scheduled to leave at 10:05 A.M. and that's exactly when we slid out of the station. The train consisted of nineteen cars, or carriages, as the Russians referred to them, and seemed to be carrying a capacity load. It appeared as though all foreigners were assigned to that one first-class car, which had a contingent of three stewardesses, only one of whom spoke a few words of English. They appeared very cold and even hostile at first, but they seemed to get friendlier as we got fur-

View from the train window

152

ther from Moscow. In fact one even had the nerve to ask me the difference between the Russian Revolution and the American Revolution and her answer was: 'After the American Revolution, things got better.'

"Being a railroad buff, I was like a kid with a new toy as I leaned out of a window which had been opened in the hallway. The heat was almost unbearable so I ignored the dirt that accompanied the breeze through the window. We never could account for the coal dust and soot as the Trans-Siberian Railway was electrified from Moscow to Lake Baikal, a distance of about 3,500 miles. I know the Russians must have thought I was crazy as I leaned out the window snapping pictures of anything and everything. How were they to know that all my life I had dreamed of making this trip and I wanted to capture every fleeting moment of it on film?

"Leaving Moscow reminded me of the Long Island Railroad with commuter stations every few miles. We couldn't figure out why the commuter trains were so crowded on Sunday. One thing we could be sure of, they weren't going to church. Shortly after leaving Moscow, we were greeted by a voice asking, 'Do you speak English?' The voice

belonged to an attractive sociologist from New York City by the name of Pat Nash.

She was equally glad to see us, as we were the only other Americans on the train. Some of the Europeans in our car did speak some English, however.

"Soon there was a knock on our door and

(Left to right) Stewardess, Winnie and Pat Nash

there stood a stewardess with two glasses of tea, or *chai* as it's called in Russia. We were continually amazed that throughout Russia they served boiling tea in glassware that was razor-thin. Perhaps the fancy pewter glass-holders prevented the glass from breaking.

"The word for restaurant in Russian is *restoran* and is spelled p-e-c-t-o-p-a-h. I have told folks, for years, that it is not the Cyrillic alphabet that is so difficult to learn, it's trying to unlearn what we have associated as sounds for our English letters all of our lives. Example: in Russia the letter p is pronounced as an r; the letter c is pronounced as an s and the letter h is pronounced as an n. Shortly before the one o'clock opening hour, we made our way to what we jokingly referred to as the *pectopah* car, pronouncing it as we would phonetically in English.

"There were only two vacant seats at a table for four, the other two being occupied by a Russian civilian and a Red Army Captain. They motioned for us to sit down and I was surprised to discover the captain spoke a few words of English. He even helped to place our orders, as the dining car personnel spoke no English at all.

"Because of the extreme heat, someone had opened the top part of a window just ahead of where we were seated. I wished I had my movie camera with me as I would have liked to have captured the expression on the face of the gentlemen seated next to my wife as his cheese turned black right before his eyes. A waitress quickly removed everything from the table, turned the tablecloth over and reset it after closing the window.

"The scenery was beautiful and there were many people standing by the tracks and waving to us as the train passed by. Every stream and pond was full of humanity trying to escape the record-breaking heat. I wanted to take more pictures, but it seemed that every time I found an interesting subject, there was something in the background that was on the no-no list for photography. I had to keep reminding

Photographing railroad stations was a no-no.

myself that this was not a free society and that I must stick to the rules governing foreigners. The presence of so many soldiers and policemen helped bring this point home, however.

"I asked the army officer many questions about the Red Army, such as how much did they pay their soldiers. He apologized and said he did not have such information. The army captain then excused himself from our table and left us with the most sincere handshake I had ever felt. I got the distinct feeling he was trying to tell me something.

"We made our way back to our car and I prepared to spend a lazy afternoon just watching the scenery flash by. The towns and villages were quite close to one another along the railway and at each one were the ever-present portraits of Lenin. In that country, that man had replaced the deity. The only signs to be seen were the ones proclaiming the accomplishments of the latest five-year plan and the promise of a glorious tomorrow that would never come.

"Photographing railroad stations was strictly taboo, so I was very careful as I surreptitiously snapped a few. We had to be told when we crossed the Urals as we had anticipated a mountain range, but we found them to be what we would consider foothills back home. However, the weather did get cooler as we came down the eastern slopes. While it was quite comfortable, the natives were complaining as they enjoyed ninety degrees above zero as much as they claimed to enjoy sixty degrees below. There had been a considerable amount of rain and many of the crops were under water.

"This was the first year that Russia had to swallow her pride and purchase wheat from America.

Perhaps I should mention that at one end of each car on the train was a coal fired boiler where passengers could

Heavy rains left many crops under water

help themselves to boiling water for instant coffee, cocoa, tea or whatever. I noticed a young fellow stoking these boilers and thought nothing of it until we entered the so-called dining car and saw this same chap peeling potatoes in spite of the fact his hands and arms were coal-black clear up to his elbows. We had to convince ourselves that as long as the potatoes were boiled we probably wouldn't get poisoned.

"If you thought Siberia was all a barren wasteland, you would be very surprised, as we were.

Siberia has flowers in spite of perma-frost

"We could have sworn we were in our own Pacific Northwest except they had many more birch trees—in fact millions of acres of them. We passed by miles and miles of evergreens with occasional clearings filled with daisies and lupine.

"Probably the most impressive scenes on the whole rail

Thousands of miles of 'Victory gardens'

trip were the individual gardens along the tracks. Can you picture over 5,000 miles of 'victory gardens'?

"The peasants were allowed to cultivate a private plot of ground and grow what they wished. Those plots appeared to be about 50 by 100 feet and were very well kept, in contrast to the collective farms.

"Nearly every square foot of every plot was utilized and nearly all were planted with potatoes. Evidently all the production went into the making of vodka, as it was almost impossible to order any potatoes for breakfast on the train. Also, it appeared as though the peasants may have been

Typical privately owned garden plot

sampling the end product when they planted their spuds. We were to learn later that about fifty percent of Russia's food production came from the two percent of the land that comprised those private plots.

"After over two days and nights on the train, we arrived at the city of Novosibirsk. We were amazed to find such a metropolis in Siberia that, at that time, had a population of 1,300,000 people. We were greeted by a beautiful tour guide, Tamara Donskikh, who really made us feel at home.

"When we reached the top of the stairs to disembark from the

Tamara, our guide in Novosibirsk

train, she called us by name, which proved what we had suspected, namely she had been advised in advance of our presence complete with description of our clothing and the like.

"Our bags were sitting on the platform and she was losing patience waiting for a porter. She finally said, "'I wonder where the porter is. Hugh, darling, will you please wait here while I summon a porter?'"

"I replied, 'yes, honey,' and I could tell that this patter was not too popular with Winnie. I tried to explain later that I was merely trying to improve international relations.

"Tamara dropped us off at our assigned hotel at 4 P.M. and announced that she would call for us at five. I told her that after over two days on the train we would have to shower but explained that for expediency we would perform that function together. She had the strangest look on her face. She was very surprised to find us ready when she returned and exclaimed,

'You know, I believe you did that.'

"She joined us for dinner and, while it was not quite as good as some we had enjoyed in Moscow, it wasn't too shabby. She had taken it upon herself to purchase tickets for us to take in the opera. She insisted that we see the performance given by the visiting Tashkent opera group. I reluctantly reimbursed her the four rubles but felt stuck for the entire evening.

"It turned out that Tamara had a fabulous sense of humor and she kept calling me 'Hugh, darling.' I wanted to tell her that I thought she was pulling my leg but didn't want to launch a course in American slang. A lot of kidding took place during dinner and later, she said, 'Hugh, darling, I think you are pulling my leg.' At the conclusion of the dinner, she insisted that we try ice cream with jam. As usual, the ice cream was better than most in the states and the jam made it a rare treat for us in Siberia. Seeing our delight with the delicacy, Tamara brought us a jar of home-made jam the next morning.

"The accommodations at the hotel were much like what we had experienced in other Soviet cities. Not exactly like Howard Johnson's or Holiday Inns but not nearly as bad as we had been led to believe. If I had to do it again, I would certainly take my own towels and some kind of plug for the bathtubs as they were always missing.

"I didn't know if I should engage her in the subject of politics, but she appeared as though, in spite of the fact she had no doubt been brainwashed, she wouldn't report us to the KGB. We assumed she had to pass rigorous loyalty tests in order to qualify as an Intourist guide.

"We asked her if she had ever seen any American movies and she quickly answered, 'Oh yes, 'They Shoot Horses, Don't They?''

"We were not familiar with that film so couldn't discuss its contents. She asked us if we'd seen any Russian flicks and I thought real quickly and took a chance on *War and Peace*. Upon our arrival back in the states, we made it a point to see *They Shoot Horses, Don't They*? We were not surprised that the Soviets allowed their citizens to see what, to them, was a propaganda piece. As I recall, it was set in the 1920s during the days of the old dance marathons when people danced until they dropped. To the communists, this was interpreted as exploitation.

"When I inquired as to whether she had seen *Dr. Zhivago*, she scowled and retorted with, 'That author was not one of our people.'

"I was beginning to feel comfortable about my conversation with Tamara in spite of the touchy subjects so cranked up my nerve to ask her, 'Tamara, I have

Opera House in Novosibirsk

been told there are about fifteen million communist party members in the Soviet Union. Is that right?'

'I've heard figures all the way from thirteen million to eighteen million,' she responded.

'Then tell me, why do the approximately 200 million citizens of this country let such a small segment rule them?'

'Simple,' Tamara said. 'They have the guns.' "I have never forgotten that statement and I can only pray that America never does either.

"She walked with us toward the opera house stopping en route to introduce us to the management of a night club where she said we would be welcome after the performance.

"She then had us stop at a bakery where she insisted we taste her favorite buns. Winnie and I about cracked up over this remark, but we didn't have the heart to fill her in on American slang. Not having any container, we had to stuff our pockets with the goodies.

"Not wanting to hang on to those baked goods during the opera, Winnie went back the short distance to the hotel to drop them off. During that interval, Tamara pulled a vial of perfume from her purse and dabbed a little behind each ear. She asked me if I liked her fragrance and my response was that if I hadn't been married, I would teach her all about capitalism. She hinted that if she hadn't been married, she would convert me to *her* way of thinking.

"She then volunteered, 'I should not be so naughty and silly. I should act like other Intourist guides,' and using her fingers, pulled down the corners of her mouth. I told her to just keep on being her light-hearted self and she would make many friends for her country. I also told her that she was such a refreshing change from the other guides we had encountered.

"Arriving at the opera house, we found we were one minute late and immediately after our arrival, the doors were closed.

"Poor Tamara, she had to sit through the first act as nobody is allowed in or out during the performance. She explained what was taking place as we didn't understand it any better in Russian than we did in Italian.

"During intermission, Tamara took us through the opera museum located just off the foyer. Speaking of the foyer, one big surprise was the size of the cloak-rooms in Siberia. I swear they were nearly as big as the auditoriums. It seems that during the winter months, the ladies of Siberia wear humongous furs and they require a lot of space.

"Tamara went on to say that on one occasion, two ladies from America asked her to see the 'Iron Curtain.' That particular opera house had a high metallic curtain so it gave Tamara great delight to show her Yankee guests the 'Iron Curtain.'

"Tamara never knew that while she bailed after the first act, we hauled anatomy after the second. Those straight back wooden seats made the seats on the train seem like luxury.

"After the opera, we headed for the night club and as nobody spoke a word of English; that was quite an experience. We sat with some Russians who were not too friendly at first, but as soon as one of them tasted one of my Pall Mall cigarettes and chattered to the others, an immediate friendship developed. We had to keep telling ourselves that for many, many years they had been brainwashed into fearing foreigners with rather dire consequences for those that disobeyed. All of our

Tamara showing Academgorodok

conversations were conducted with drawings on paper napkins. I recall them drawing a picture of a space ship then clasping my hand and writing 1975. They said '*Apollo*, good show, good show,' so I responded with, '*Sputnik, Sputnik*, good show, good show.' Indeed 1975 was the year when Americans and Russians conducted a joint space mission...

"The next day Tamara appeared with that jar of home-made berry jam which later made us very popular in the dining car on the train. She had commandeered a Volkswagen bus with an Intourist driver and they took us several miles out of the city to a small city known as *Academ Gorodok* or, in English, Academy Township.

"It consisted of a sprawling campus of many buildings like various American colleges and universities. She explained that it had an enrollment of over 100,000 students. It seems that they used to give an aptitude test to all the high-school seniors in the Soviet Union and those with the highest marks were given scholarships to this institution of higher learning in Siberia. Their four-year courses lasted five years as the students were required to work one year in public service, usually on collective farms.

"Later, Tamara accompanied us to lunch at a shopping center. During our drive back to the big city, Tamara asked us many questions about where we worked and life in America. I didn't realize it, but she had whispered to Winnie and asked her if it would be possible for us to purchase and send a couple of wigs to her. Tamara had a beautiful voice and entertained us with her renditions of '*This Land is My Land*' and '*We Shall Overcome*.' She knew every word. Seemed strange to hear the latter being sung in a communist country.

"Later in the day, Tamara took us to a crowded beach where hundreds of folks were enjoying a swim in their great inland sea, the lake formed by the damming of the Ob River. I jokingly told Tamara that I was going to refer to my photography of this episode as 'Obscene.' We promised to correspond with our lovely guide and send her copies of the photographs we had taken, which we did.

"After a twenty-four hour break that gave us a chance to bathe and enjoy a change of menus, we again boarded the train for the two-day ride to Irkutsk."

CHAPTER 19

The next morning found some new faces in the 'Cultural Exchange Group' at Resurrection Retirement Resort. Among them was one that belonged to Nellie Rue, an attractive middle-aged lady that was touring all the facilities in the Resurrection Chain. Her opening remarks certainly got the attention of Hugh Williams as she promised to elucidate on the subject of immigration.

"Back in your day, Mr. Williams, as I recall, one of your pet peeves was the fact that American security was as loose as a goose.

"Not now. After 9/11 the INS finally got the message from the terrorists and really tightened the screws on visas. When the American public was made aware of the fact that the INS issued over 55,000 visas to Middle Eastern Nationals, other than Israelis, in the first six months following 9/11 they went ballistic.

"This precipitated a complete overhaul of America's entire immigration policy. Back in double-aught two, we had no idea of where any of our foreign visitors were located and it was oh-so easy for visitors to simply disappear. When it was disclosed that extension visas were issued to terrorists *after* they skyjacked the planes that crashed into the World Trade Center and the Pentagon, Uncle Sam finally decided to get tough. After years of squabbling, congress finally admitted something had to be none.

"Now, even student visas expire at the end of thirty days, at which time, the recipients must report to the INS agent assigned to their file. Should the visitor fail to do so, a warrant is issued for his or her arrest and they are subject to immediate deportation.

"In addition, visitors must provide addresses and phone numbers where they may be reached at all times. Failure to do so may also subject the visa holder to deportation. Such penalties are in addition to the $100 per day fine levied against these delinquent visitors. It's amazing how such measures have cut down on the number of illegal immigrants we have in America nowadays. Oh yes, there were cries of 'police state,' etc. etc. but when a nation's very survival is at stake, harsh actions required harsh *reactions*.

"While we're on the subject of illegal immigrants, about this time folks wised up to the fact that millions of illegals were receiving the best of medical care along with dental services. This was in addition to welfare, food stamps, subsidized housing and who knows what? Indeed, it has been claimed that some of these 'guests' even received automobiles. With millions of our own citizens who had paid taxes all of their lives unable to afford such luxuries, there arose a bitterness toward many of the immigrants who had learned to milk the system.

"Examples of aliens who could not read nor write a single word of English and yet who possessed driver's licenses began to tick off more and more of the populace, and the pressure forced many states to discontinue the practice of giving the drivers' tests in multiple languages. I knew first-hand that many hard-working seniors employed at menial tasks could not afford to have dental work done. When they were able to save enough for an appointment, many times they were forced to wait while so-called refugees were getting the most expensive work done and paying for it with state medical certificates. To add insult to injury, the taxpayers were footing the bill to pay the escorts for these freeloaders. Some disgruntled citizens swore that the refugees were even given gold fillings in their teeth.

"For years the liberal press seemed reluctant to publicize these injustices, but when they finally succumbed to the public pressure heads began to roll.

"If the subject hasn't already been covered, I'd like to bring Mr. Williams up to speed on the issue of language. Back in 2012, the Common Sense Party garnered a lot of votes by having an English language plank in their platform. No longer will most government agencies print any documents in languages other than English.

"By now, I suppose I have worn out my welcome so I'll surrender the microphone to our knowledgeable professor for more of his fascinating yarns about the former Soviet Union."

Hugh Williams was wide-awake and picked up on the cue instantly. "Let's see, I believe we were back on the train en route from Novosibirsk to the Lake Baikal Area of Siberia.

"In Novosibirsk, we had purchased over 100 post cards and stamps and spent much of the next leg of our journey writing to our friends back home. Upon checking later, we found every card went through and they took an average of eleven days. We had also purchased an atlas and, although it was printed in Russian, we could look at the name on a railway station and then find it in the book. I immediately became the tour guide for our car as people were constantly asking me, 'Where are we?'

"I liked to think we had smuggled a tape recorder into the Soviet Union—that's another no-no—but, as I said earlier, we had not been checked upon arrival as everyone we talked to had been. Those caught with tape recorders had them sealed at the border and that seal had better be intact when they left the country. I should also mention that a tourist was allowed to bring one Bible into the country, but they had better have it when they exited.

"The stewardesses took one look at my recorder and said, in broken English, 'What American progress!' I didn't have the heart to tell her it was made in Japan. Before I left home I had taped an hour of a country-western radio station and I thought those girls were going to wear out the tape. They especially enjoyed the singing commercials. Those Russians really dug those country-western songs. After they overcame their stage fright, they sang Russian songs for me and were quite good considering they had no accompaniment. They insisted that Winnie and I dance rock and roll in the companionway.

"Arriving at Irkutsk, a city of over half a million people, we were again greeted by a very efficient Intourist guide. This was truly a city of contrasts with many new apartment houses but, as in other Soviet cities, much of the population was housed in log cabins. In some parts of the city, the modern articulated trolley buses and streetcars looked out of keeping with their ancient surroundings.

"When we asked if we might visit a typical Russian home, we were greeted with, 'That would not be possible.'

"A driving rain made our sightseeing tour less enjoyable than it might have been. I vividly recall being taken to a cemetery, right downtown that contained the graves of 113 heroes of the Great Patriotic War as the Russians referred to World War II.

Articulated bus in Irkutsk

"We thought the setting was strange as it was right next door to the city library. Looking out of our hotel window, I was able to photograph what looked to be a peasant lady sweeping the sidewalks with a broom fashioned from sticks.

Cemetery of the Heroes in Irkutsk

"A couple more baths, a sightseeing excursion and some shopping plus a good bed in what they called a first-class hotel—then it was back on the train for the three days and nights required to get to Khabarovsk. Now the scenery became more spectacular as we followed the shore of Lake Baikal for hours. That is the world's largest body of fresh water and contains one-fifth of the world's entire fresh water supply. The time seemed to pass all too quickly as each time we stopped over, we were greeted by a different crew on the next day's train and we had to go through the tape recorder bit with each one.

Lady sweeping sidewalk with broom of twigs

"While it was against the law to tip in the Soviet Union and they would never openly accept one, we found that a few kopecks left under our plates in the dining car certainly seemed to improve the service. Fortunately, I had a good supply of my company's ballpoint pens and discovered that those certainly helped to

Our hotel in Irkutsk

seal a friendship in Russia.

"Perhaps this would be a good time, at the risk of being redundant, to reiterate to my audience that all the way across the Soviet Union, we were constantly viewing communist propaganda signs, banners and statues.

I won't go so far as to say the trip was boring, but the villages all seemed to look alike. I kept telling myself that I was viewing America circa 1900.

Communist signs proclaiming five-year plan

*One of the ever-present
pictures of Lenin*

*We couldn't escape
Lenin's gaze*

Lenin had replaced the Deity in Soviet Union

Typical village in Siberia. They lost 75 years.

"I should also point out this segment of the journey was powered by steam.

"That fact, coupled with the beautifully colored railroad rolling stock would make a rail fan think he had died and gone to heaven.

This portion of journey was powered by steam

171

Russia had lots of colorful railway equipment

Another colorful Russian locomotive

Peasant ladies selling chicken on platform

"At most stops, there were peasants on the platform selling everything from salads to butterflied chickens.

"One enterprising peasant lady had a baby buggy filled with *piva*—beer—covered with ice. At some of the smaller villages, the locals would literally swarm the dining car to purchase such delicacies as oranges and chocolate.

More ladies selling salads, veggies, fish, etc.

*One of many kiosks along
the Trans-Siberian*

Free enterprise, Soviet style

We saw a couple of examples of what was as close to free enterprise as existed in Soviet Russia of 1972.

"I have always regretted not getting the recipe for the dill pickles I purchased from a peasant lady as they had to be the world's best.

"During the next portion of the trip the railroad followed close to the border between Russia and China. It looked like an armed camp with soldiers standing with rifles at each end of every bridge and tunnel. At this point, I was careful with my cameras. One man in our car wasn't, and he spent the night in jail in Khabarovsk. It seems he was a journalist for a French publication. We never saw him again until we were on the steamer bound for Japan. He didn't take a single picture I'm sure until he was safely on the

*These had to be the world's
best dill pickles*

ground in Yokohama.

"While passing near the Chinese border, I stayed up until the wee small hours so I could possibly get a view of the lights from that country. I recall getting off the train and asking one of the stewardesses if I was looking at China and how far it was. She asked me why I asked such questions and gave a signal, which alerted soldiers and I caught a glimpse of them approaching me with rifles. I remarked, 'I just remembered it's way past my bedtime,' and jumped aboard the train without touching a step. Winnie was waiting at our compartment door and exclaimed, 'Didn't you hear me knocking on the window and pointing to the soldiers?' I said, 'No, but once I saw them I probably set a new long and high-jump record.

"It was during this portion of the trip that Winnie got the curse. She had been so proud of her planning and had suffered that malady just before she left Corfu to meet me in Copenhagen. She just knew she would be in ship-shape until we reached Tokyo.

"What an experience. She called for the stewardess and holding her English/Russian dictionary, pointed to the word for month, followed by the word for sick. The poor gal just didn't understand or 'pony my you nyet' as they say it in Russian. Winnie finally pointed to the part of her anatomy that was the subject of discussion and suddenly the girl made a bee-line down the corridor. I felt this might be a good time for me to retreat to the *pectopah* car for a tall cool *piva*.

"When I returned, our compartment was full of Russian femininity all trying to talk at the same time. I glanced at the lower bunk and couldn't keep a straight face. There had to be what looked like a bale of cotton, complete with the seeds, being fashioned into some gauze that could have passed for a bed sheet.

"If it hadn't been so embarrassing, I would have suggested we submit it to the Guinness Book of Records. No way could any lady have worn that get-up and still have been able to walk unless, of course, she was extremely bow-legged. The incident did, however, remind me to include a note of caution in my journal to the effect that feminine hygiene products were not readily available in Russia and that the Soviet Union didn't have drug stores on every corner.

"We arrived in the city of Khabarovsk in the evening and welcomed a good night's sleep without the rock and roll of the train. The next day presented us with some wonderful sightseeing—including a visit to a fantastic zoo where we viewed the famous Siberian white tigers—and some shopping. As in the other cities we had visited, when I asked if we might visit a typical Russian home or apartment, we were greeted with the same standard response: 'Oh, we're so sorry, but time does not permit such visits.'

"That evening, we again boarded the train for the 500-mile overnight trip to Nahodka. I'll admit that I took a tranquilizer that last morning, as I was so afraid that the customs officers would find my tape recorder and maybe even confiscate my film.

"For this portion of the journey, the Russians really put their best foot forward. We couldn't believe the nice curtains in the dining car, linen napkins, the silverware and watermelon.

"They even served potatoes for breakfast. They had a rack with a lot of literature printed in English. A sign said 'Souvenirs. Please take some.' That I did, and it all turned out to be a lot of communist propaganda, some of which was quite subtle.

Fancy dining car on last leg of journey

"The next morning, as we approached Vladivostok, our car was cut from the herd and shunted to Nakhodka. That came as no surprise to us as we had been aware for quite some time that no Westerners were allowed into Vladivostok for it contained, what the Russians wanted us to believe, the world's largest naval base. Our rail car was taken right to the pier where we were to clear customs and immigration. We had made the acquaintance of a couple from East Germany and tears flowed down their cheeks as they informed us that this was as far as they were allowed to go. They were still staring at us as the ship left the pier.

"For some unknown reason, Customs just looked at our declaration, checked our money and waved us on to the ship—MS Baikal—that was going to take us to Japan. Everyone else was checked, and I do mean really checked. By this time, there were seven Americans on the train and as I passed by one of our newly formed friends, a professor from the University of Pennsylvania, was virtually in tears. She pleaded, 'Please Hugh, help me. They don't want to let me pass.' I yelled back, 'They told me to get on the ship and that's what I'm going to do. I will see that Winnie is safely ensconced in our cabin and I'll come back for you.' When I came back down the gangway, a soldier would not let me get back to the stranded professor but fortunately she convinced them she was not a smuggler. It seems she forgot to declare a pendant when she entered the Soviet

Train station and steamship pier in Nakhodka

Union and some smart-ass customs guy thought he saw an opportunity to expropriate some jewelry. Her cries attracted the attention of others so the guy decided it might be best that he pick on some other passenger.

"When I started taking photos of the ship from the pier, the soldier yelled '*nyet*' and pointed to the top of

Band playing 'Going to Kansas City', on ship

the gangway. He motioned that I should take pictures from the deck, not the dock. This made absolutely no sense to me as I could photograph many vessels from the deck loading war material for Vietnam while none could be seen from the pier.

"As we pulled away from the dock, the Russian ship's band was out on deck playing '*Going to Kansas City.*'

"That evening, during the dance in the lounge, they played '*Lara's Theme.*' I asked them if they knew the significance of that tune and they replied, 'No, we just know it's a popular song in the West.' I wasn't about to go through the bit about *Dr. Zhivago* again.

"That portion of the journey required two days and nights plus about five hours but it was very enjoyable as the accommodations were the best we had seen anywhere in the Soviet Union. Part of that voyage was very rough and when I went to the restaurant for breakfast, there were only two of us there. The other passenger was carrying a red passport, so I knew she was Russian but the nature of this voyage also told me she probably was bi-lingual. I enjoyed conversation with her during breakfast.

"The ship had air-conditioned staterooms, a beautiful bar with cold drinks, a fancy ballroom and dining rooms where we could actually order food like we were accustomed to back home.

"Another no-no is arriving in Yokohama at 5 P.M. on a Friday. I do believe it took at least two hours by taxi to Tokyo. All across Siberia, Winnie and I kept talking about what we were going to order when we got back to civilization. Every time we discussed food, we started drooling for the steaks we were going to devour when we reached Japan. As luck would have it, my boss, being very considerate, had booked us into the Imperial Hotel. In the few seconds it took to get from the taxi to the door of the hotel, we became soaking wet. Talk about humidity.

"When we went to the dining room after checking in, we were informed we could not be served as I wasn't wearing a tie. Was I mad? My memory of Pearl Harbor came back and we stomped out. Our fabulous first meal back in civilization consisted of a cheeseburger and a chocolate shake but, would you believe it, it tasted like a banquet.

"The trip between Moscow and Yokohama had to have been the world's biggest travel bargain. When one considers that it took over ten days and nights to travel the 7,000 miles and the ticket price included a private compartment on the train, a private compartment on the ship and all meals, the price of $319 was indeed very reasonable.

"Upon our return, we gave the following advice to Russian bound travelers:

1 "Try to learn a few Russian words. It's nice to be able to ask such things as 'where are the restrooms?' Incidentally, this advice still applied during my last trip to Russia in October of 2000, two months prior to my accident.

2 "Be patient: if you think the wheels of bureaucracy turn slowly in America, your experiences in Russia will make you appreciate our 'slow service.'

3   "Don't think of a trip to Russia as a vacation, it's an adventure. If you are fastidious and cannot stand a little dirt and inconvenience, both you and your country are better off if you stay home.

"Aside from the ballet, opera and circus, my wife hated that adventure and when asked her opinion of it she was quick to respond, 'As far as I'm concerned, three weeks under communism was about twenty-one days too long.'

"Being a political animal, when I was asked to define the biggest difference between communism and capitalism, with only one choice, I had to say the right to own property. Of course there are many more, such as freedom of speech, press, assembly and certainly free enterprise. They did have one plank in their constitution, however, that might bear looking at: 'He that shall not work, neither shall he eat.'

"Well, ladies and gentlemen, you now know as much about Russia and the Trans-Siberians Railroad as I did at that time. By now many of you have no doubt heard that yours truly made nine more journeys to that part of the world but that's a different chapter, or should I say chapters?

"I know we have many more folks who are eager to participate in our round-table discussions and just because I ran out of Russian yarns doesn't signal an immediate cessation of our wonderful exchanges. In fact, I have a couple of vignettes that I will share with you now.

"As I recall, during one of our tours of Moscow, we found some flyers blowing around the streets. I picked one up and asked our guide what they were selling. She examined it and a look of shock came over her face. Why she translated it to us, I'll never know but she added it was very dangerous for anyone to get caught with such literature. It merely asked the question: Why does a Russian have to work for three months to earn enough to buy a new suit of clothes while his American counterpart works only three days for the same amount?"

Before the class could be dismissed, another hand shot up and the owner of same identified herself as Rita Wendel.

"If you don't mind, I am leaving town tomorrow and would like to insert a 'quickie' at this juncture. I know it wasn't on your original list, but I wonder if you are interested in what has taken place in the field of charity?

"Over the years, when the various states demanded that charities file statements with them and folks began learning how much of their donations went to fund-raising, many charities had to change their tune. Perhaps one of the biggest rhubarbs took place right here in Portland, Oregon when their United Way decided to drop the Boy Scouts of America from their list of recipients. It at least accomplished one goal: it took the politics out of charities. It still didn't stop the government from playing Robin Hood with our money, however."

"Thanks so much, Rita for that unexpected but welcome contribution. Sorry to hear that you won't be able to continue this course."

CHAPTER 20

Word had spread like wild-fire throughout the facility about the new round-table discussion format and those who had been reluctant to participate, all of a sudden, had many opinions and they all wanted to get their words in edgewise. Hugh Williams opened the session with the announcement that he had been informed by staff that a special visitor had flown in from Tucson and was to be introduced. Ms. Leslie Pegg had the honor of being the 'Poster Lady' of the Common Sense Party. It was she who came up with the party's slogan: "A Promise Made is a Debt Unpaid." She was a short lovable Jewish lady who had captured the hearts of even some of the loyal opposition.

After an introduction, a few words of wisdom followed by a warm round of applause, Ms. Pegg accompanied Hugh down the hall for a little 'side bar'.

"Mr. Williams, I'm so thrilled to meet you. Are you aware you are now known nationally and the whole country is following your progress? You're not too bad looking. Do you suppose we could meet sometime when you're not conversing with a couple hundred people?"

"I think that might be arranged, Ms...may I call you Leslie? As you know, it's been over twenty years since I've known any female companionship so I may not know quite how to act."

"Don't worry, Hugh, I'll coach you. You may recall they used to say it's like riding a bicycle, once you learn, you never forget."

As planned, Ms. Pegg stopped by on Saturday to pick up Hugh Williams and he had a weekend at the Oregon Coast he'd never forget. Promises, promises? Yes, lots of promises, but no debts left unpaid.

Talk about bright-eyed and bushy-tailed, those words best described the professor on Monday morning. He even sounded better and if the class hadn't guessed that he'd had his pump primed, a grin from ear to ear disclosed his not too secret secret. He announced they had definitely reached the point where he felt they should change the format to round table discussions or be forced to offer a 'graduate' course.

It didn't take long for all participants to learn that "Professor" William's coffee klatches had become really interactive with quickie subjects. All members of the audience were encouraged to contribute pertinent information concerning any and all significant occurrences during the last twenty years.

When the next exchange was called to order, Hugh Williams was pleased to see a forest of upraised arms when he called for volunteers. He did a double take as he couldn't believe the longest arm on the tallest lady belonged to his daughter Kim. When she introduced herself, she received a nice round of applause as she marched right up to the microphone.

"This is rat on daddy day," she announced. "How many of you would like to get the real skinny on your professor?" The 'class' responded in a heartbeat and there was no way Hugh could escape.

"What if I was to tell you that Mr. Williams was a candidate for Congress? Well, as a matter of fact, he was a candidate on four occasions in the Third District right across the river in Washington." There were murmurs throughout the hall as some folks expressed surprise while others said I could have told you so. One resident said, "It figures, after all didn't he say he did stand-up comedy? Isn't that about the same as politics?"

Hugh overheard that remark and just had to respond. "They also say that politics is the world's second oldest profession and not too different from the first. Okay, Kim, honey, as long at it's my turn in the barrel, you might as well give them the whole nine yards."

"Well, dad, while digging through your papers I came across one of your old 'slim jim' handouts. Among other things, it describes you as a compassionate conservative and that was long before either one of the Bush presidents came upon the scene. You also used a slogan that I have always liked: 'The government that governs best, governs least.' Now, if your 'students' can bear with me, I'll list the planks in your campaign platform." With that, she wrote on the white board:

- Charity begins at home.
- More local control.
- Not one penny for foreign aid while any American is homeless and/or hungry through no fault of his or her own.
- Reinstate the sales tax deduction from Federal Income Tax.
- Restore IRAs for everyone.
- Social Security should be funded on the same sound basis as private insurance
- Social Security income should not be taxed.
- Unlimited earnings for Social Security recipients.
- No federal funding for abortions.
- Repeal portions of the Jones Act to enable our sawmills to better compete.
- Toughen laws on crime and drugs.

- Capital punishment for traitors, murderers, cop killers, molesters and rapists.

- Remove all commercial fishing from the Columbia River.

- A flat rate of 10% for Federal Income Tax.

- Better accounting of federal funds.

"There, how does that grab ya'? Now what do you have to say for yourself?"

"I guess I was just ahead of the times, but I don't regret a minute of it. I hope the 'class' accepts those planks in the context of the times they were used in my campaigns. If memory serves me accurately, they were last used way back in 1988.

"About as close as I ever got to the national political scene was getting elected as an Alternate to the GOP National Convention in Detroit in 1980 and as a Delegate to the Dallas Convention in 1984. I did, however, get a chance to meet a lot of the party hierarchy notables such as Goldwater, Nixon, Reagan and the first President Bush—he and I became friends. I made it a point to bring him a twelve-pack of Blitz Weinhard's Private Reserve beer whenever we met.

"But Kim, dear, you blew my cover. Now people will label me as a conservative."

"You gotta' be kidding, Daddy. Shall I tell them that once I overheard you say that to you the John Birch Society was a left-wing organization?" This brought chuckles from the 'class' and one could hear the older folks trying to explain to the younger generations about that organization way back in the sixties.

"To your credit though, Dad, I also heard you campaign for a stronger Social Security system. I believe you also said you wanted the same things as the liberals—health care and education for all—but you wanted to know who was going to pay for it."

"Thanks a lot, honey…I think. Now I feel like the naked emperor. We've wasted a lot of time on my sordid past and it's way past time that we give another of our researchers the opportunity to lay some new subject on us.

"Next?" Hugh asked into the microphone. "Wait a minute, that's me. Now I suppose many of you are ready to step back again in time to Communist Russia, circa 1972 or perhaps I should say liberated Russia circa 1991.

"As I recall, I received a phone call during the wee small hours of the morning one day in July of 1991. I was told I was famous in Novosibirsk as it seems that Tamara had been talking non-stop about my visit of 1972. The voice asked me if I had received their letter and when I answered in the negative, he asked if there was a place where he could send a fax. I gave him the number of my local printer and he explained they had sent an invitation for me to journey to Novosibirsk to teach capitalism at the newly formed Siberian Teen-agers School of Business.

"My poor wife, Winnie, was on her death bed so I informed them that I couldn't possibly make such a journey at that time. I lost Winnie on July 30 to the ravages of lung cancer. I knew that Winnie would have wanted me to go and go I did in late September. I must say that it was an experience I'll never forget; I thought I had died and gone to Heaven, standing in the October Revolution Palace beneath a statue of Lenin and teaching free-market economy.

"And you thought I had no more tales about Russia, didn't you?" asked Hugh. "At this time, I'd like to share with you an incident that occurred during one of our sightseeing tours in Moscow. Our guide took us up to Moscow University that is located on the Lenin Hills overlooking the city.

"It had a fantastic view looking across the Moscow River to the huge stadium that held over 100,000 people. With my movie camera,

I started sweeping the panoramic view when a policeman tapped me on the shoulder and said, in no uncertain terms. '*Nyet.*' Ooops—while photographing a ski jump just below our observation point, it didn't occur to me that there was a bridge in the background.

"I asked our guide if she would be kind enough to translate my remarks to the officer. 'Please tell him that I think it is stupid to be so paranoid about such things as bridges as my country has a satellite that flies over every hour and twenty minutes with a camera that was so high tech that it could read the brand name on the cigarette he held in his hand. I can only assume that she must have translated my message literally for he had the strangest look on his face."

University of Moscow on Lenin Hills…Moscow

CHAPTER 21

"Take a number," was Hugh's opening remark at the next day's continuing saga of the now-famous seminar exchange. What a contrast from the first sessions where almost everyone was almost as shy as a little girl on her first day of kindergarten. Indeed one of the participants brought some of the members of her Toastmasters Club so they could hear some of the 'speeches' delivered from folks who had never even given an "icebreaker."

Hugh led off the morning session with a reference to being "politically correct."

"Is that idiotic fad still in vogue?" He asked. "I recall that before my accident, I predicted it could be the ruination of our country.

"I don't suppose many of you here recall a TV program called *Politically Incorrect.* Way back in 1999 I was a guest on that show and they never asked me back. It seems they didn't appreciate a conservative in Hollywood. If anyone is really serious about viewing that show they might check with ABC and ask for a copy of that show's episode number 1999-500.

"Back around the turn of the century, the liberals and greenies hung their hats on being politically correct. It was their crutch and excuse for every lame-brained government spending program under the sun. Surely the country has wised up since then. You tell me we were attacked on September 11, 2001 so it must be assumed we tightened up our borders since then."

"No way," came a voice from the back row, "or should I say at least not at that time?" He introduced himself as Carl Donald and gave his occupation as just plain retired conservative.

"Back in about two-aught ten, the citizens demanded that we crack down on illegal immigrants. The president issued a decree to the effect America would embark on a zero-tolerance policy toward illegal immigrants. A program was launched known as 'Operation Clean Sweep' or OCS. All illegal aliens were required to report to the nearest INS office to be registered, finger-printed and undergo a thorough background check. Those who failed to register or who couldn't pass muster, were immediately deported. It was estimated that the number of illegals dropped from approximately twenty million to less than three million.

"There was the usual screaming from the bleeding-heart liberals, but the president responded with the edict that we were in survivor mode and when it came to the question of terrorists or us, we opted for the latter.

"Our immigration laws were not only strengthened, at long last, they were enforced. No longer were immigrants allowed to come to America to become wards of the state. Even back in your day, Hugh, when a U.S. citizen sponsored a foreign visitor, they were required to sign a document to the effect the citizen would be responsible for all the visitor's needs while on US territory".

"Been there, done that," interrupted Hugh. "Back in 1993, I took a terrible chance by sponsoring three Russians and I signed such a document. Little did I know that Uncle Sam was not enforcing this provision. I kept thinking about the possibility of one of them getting ill and me having to pay the bill. It was later that I learned that so many immigrants were signing affidavits to the effect they were in good health but upon arrival in this country, many had to be hospitalized at taxpayer's expense.

"I also discovered that some churches were sponsoring immigrants but somehow they either didn't sign such agreements or they weren't enforced. They gave these new members of their congregations funds to tide them over until they received their first welfare checks then they became wards of the state. The Libs were still preaching separation of church and state, while the U.S. Government was actually building congregations for certain churches, mostly Baptist, Pentecostal and Adventists.

"For years, we taught our youngsters that America is great because we are a nation of laws. It sounded a bit hypocritical for several administrations to reward so many lawbreakers with the granting of amnesty.

"When Uncle Sam announced a get tough policy regarding the enforcement of the provisions governing the sponsorship of immigrants, the religious persecuted flow dribbled down to a trickle. Sorry for the interruption," Hugh apologized, "but I simply had to interject those memories while they were fresh in my mind.

"Oh, by the way, just for the record, if you want an update of the three Russians I sponsored and alluded to earlier, two of them were here for just a month or two and the third, a lovely lady from Siberia, is happily married, gainfully employed and is now an American citizen. She never received one dime of charity nor did she ever receive one cent of our taxpayer's money."

"Things have definitely changed for the better," responded Mr. Donald. "It took only a few incidents where the sponsor had to bear the expense of open heart surgery for others to get the message. That, coupled with the fact immigrants could no longer get all the freebies, such as health care, made all but the wealthiest have second thoughts about sticking their necks out to sponsor foreigners."

"That's great, but what about the INS and our loose border policy?" Hugh asked. "Well, in spite of the screams from the Libs about our deporting students who failed to report to their INS 'probation' officers, Uncle Sugar tightened our borders to a point where they almost resembled the iron curtain of your day. The libs had another cow when congress approved funds for erecting a fence along our southern border but the enactment of strict laws fining employers one hundred thousand dollars per offense the hiring of undocumented aliens made the erection of a fence virtually unnecessary.

"When it came to racial profiling, you can imagine the chagrin of those same liberals when the official response to their bitching was: 'Bullshit, we are through stopping ninety-year-old black ladies in wheel chairs when we're more interested in folks of Arabic extraction. After all, our police have engaged in 'racial profiling' for years. When they issue an APB—all points bulletin—they have no qualms about describing the suspect as white male, black female, etc. They describe the wanted party that allegedly committed the crime and the official position of the United States Government is that we are looking for criminals also but when we know they are from the Middle East, we are not going to profile Japanese midgets. However, if we have reason to believe anyone is connected with the Al Qaeda, we will arrest them regardless if they are purple, pink, polka-dot or plaid."

"Thank you very much, Mr. Donald. I'm so glad to learn that Uncle Sam has wised up when it comes to immigrants."

"Hold it" came a voice from a freckle faced red headed lady who hadn't said a word during any of the previous sessions.

"Allow me to introduce myself. I answer to the handle of Mona Janney and before you get too far removed from the subject of 'politically incorrect,' I'd like to share with you what our ladies club has been up to. We refuse to refer to our leader as 'chair.' Damn it, she is the chair *woman* and we are encouraging the men folks to revert to chair *man* in their organizations. As for all the asinine sexual harassment suits, we think the whole concept stinks. It has succeeded only in greatly reducing a lady's chance to receive compliments. Someone once remarked that a lady would spend hours trying to look seductive then slap any guy that tried to seduce her. While we are not trying to get seduced, we don't think it's a crime for a man to tell us we look stunning in certain outfits."

"Gee, what a pleasant interruption. Thanks Mona," remarked Hugh.

"I know that my students are under the impression I am all out of Russian tales, but quite the opposite is true. As I related my adventures of so many years ago, I was constantly reminded of various vignettes that had not been included in my journal.

"You may recall that at the start of our trip on the Trans-Siberian from Moscow, I informed you that there was only one other American on the train. I believe I identified her as Pat Nash, a sociologist from New York City. She had explained that she had been invited to present a paper on sociology at a conference in Kiev. She said she had been ignored and even ostracized and I do believe she had second thoughts about socialism in general.

"One day when she joined my wife and me in the 'dining car,' she asked me what all those small logs were on the many flat cars we passed. I explained that we were passing through the 'taiga' which was comprised of about 2,000 miles of conifers' generously interspersed with millions of birch trees. I asked her if she had noticed that the toilets seats in each end of the car were wooden. When she answered in the affirmative, I responded with: 'Congratulations, Pat, you are now a charter member of the Birch John Society.' Evidently, she did not see the humor in that remark as her grin didn't compare with my laughter.

"Little did we realize at that time that the next summer she would journey all the way from New York City out to the State of Washington to stay a few days with us. I recall how thrilled she was when I allowed her to pick the corn for our dinner one evening. I had to show her how and Winnie and I came to the conclusion that, being from Manhattan, she had never picked an ear of corn in her life."

Much to everyone's surprise, including Hugh's, the next day's venue was changed to a nearby building that was known as the Sunny Valley Grange Hall. This was done to accommodate some classes from the local Middle School. This shift was made only after a promise that the proceedings would be video taped so the staff members who had so many hours invested would not lose a chapter. At first, the sixth grade youngsters acted bored and were quite inattentive, however the older kids, especially those in the eighth grade were actually taking notes. Perhaps it may have been because their instructor warned them that their next social studies test would incorporate some of the material covered at this informal class.

They seemed especially interested in learning about Russia under communism and the session consisted mostly of viewing the many slides that were taken of that trip of 1972.

During the breaks, they flocked around Hugh, each with a zillion questions about the Russia of fifty years ago.

'Professor' Williams finally promised that he would see to it that their school would receive a video of the entire exchange from day one. He also saw to it that a copy of that video was brought back to the rest home to enable those unable to attend the Grange Hall meeting to keep abreast of the 'course.'

CHAPTER 22

It was decided that it might be a good idea to dove-tail the next session with the Sunday brunch held each week and which was attended by many relatives of the residents at Resurrection Resort. Many of these visitors had heard of the cultural exchanges, but their employment precluded their ability to attend. While the brunch was normally scheduled from nine to one, by 8:30, the dining room was packed to the rafters.

After being introduced, Hugh Williams gave a 'quickie' overview of the subjects the participants had covered and promised that the meeting would conclude with a series of slide shows about Russia in 1972 and subsequent trips to that country.

"Some of you may recall that I mentioned early in the series, that I had made more trips to Russia. You will note in the slides, the vast difference between 1972 and 2000. I think you will be especially interested in the 1991 series when yours truly was invited to Novosibirsk in Siberia to teach capitalism upon the fall of communism.

"For the benefit of the many first-timers we have in attendance today, I should mention that in previous sessions, one of many subjects discussed, in addition to my Russia travelogue, required an entire session. We finally reached a point where the many subjects that remained on the agenda didn't require a whole session. It was decided that our forum would be changed to one more like a round-table discussion. Thus, we have several folks talking about a lot of things today. "How many volunteer speakers do we have today?" asked Hugh and it appeared that at least a dozen hands reached skyward. "Well, it appears as though we are going to have to draw straws after all."

"I believe I got the long straw," remarked a middle-aged gentleman who identified himself as Colin James, a nephew of one of the retirement home's oldest residents. He explained that as he was self-employed in the house inspection profession, he was his own boss and was able to schedule many of his appointments around the daily coffee hours.

"I realize this wasn't on your original list, but one of my favorite pet peeves has been truth in advertising, or the lack thereof. I got really ticked off when I used to hear ads on TV tell me they offered a given product that was a $99 value but was available for about $19.95. I maintained that if the value was $99, that is what it would have sold for. I also lost patience with ads that repeatedly listed the price of a product but failed to mention 'plus shipping and handling'. I decided to boycott such products and apparently others did too as it was about 2011 when the wise advertisers decided to quote prices delivered to the home.

"One of the biggest improvements in advertising came about when it was ruled that politicians could no longer sling mud. If they charged their opponent with accusations that were untrue, they could be sued for slander. Newspapers had to scrutinize letters to the editor and when one writer referred to another writer's letter claiming they had made a certain statement, it had better be there. Some papers adopted a plan to print letters just as they were submitted, complete with all misspelling, dangling participles, etc…with the exception, of course, of any swearing or profanity. Of course, a disclaimer appeared on each editorial page.

"I recall that there used to be a judge that was a member of my Rotary Club and he remarked that some folks whom he had to sentence to jail couldn't put two words together to construct a sentence. Later he would read a letter to the editor, signed by that incarcerated individual, which looked like a literary masterpiece. It was during an editor's talk before our club that we all learned that the editorial staff doctored all letters and even changed the meaning of some before they were published. Many of us remarked that for years, the amount of credence we lent those letters was in direct proportion to the spelling, grammar and punctuation."

"I'm sure glad you brought that subject up, Mr. James," interjected Hugh Williams. "I used to feel the same way but the ad that really twisted my shorts came out in the late nineties. I used to hear a man tell us that the housing on his vacuum cleaner was guaranteed for ten *long* years. The very next ad, sponsored by an Oil Heating Institute, advised me that the new oil furnaces were so efficient they would pay for themselves in a few *short* years. Talk about an insult to one's intelligence. I called a dealer and had them come out to remove my oil furnace and replace it with an electric unit with a heat pump."

"Another of my pet peeves was the constant misuse of the words better and best. I made it a practice to send a certificate to the sponsor of such ads announcing they were given a Bone-Head Grammar award for stating they liked a product better or best instead of more or most."

It appeared as though the guests enjoyed the discussion and slides so much Resurrection Resort would have to trot out the dinner menu.

CHAPTER 23

Athe next meeting of the "Educational Exchange Club," when Professor Williams announced he was coming into the home stretch, a group immediately started making plans for a last hurrah dinner.

Most participants eagerly accepted the change in format and looked forward to each session. Perhaps it was the element of surprise that they enjoyed, not knowing who would respond with what subject.

"Okay. Who got the next longest straw?" Mr. Williams asked. With that, the first hand to be raised was on the arm attached to the body of one Hardy James, a man who was a complete stranger to the group. He announced that he was just visiting Portland on a business call in connection with his computer business back in New England and happened to see a blurb in the *Oregonian* about the now famous coffee klatches being conducted at Resurrection so decided to sit in on a session.

"Has the subject of 'The power of one' been covered?" When Hugh answered in the negative, Hardy explained that back in the early part of the century, many folks discovered they didn't have to have a million dollars to hire a high-priced Madison Avenue advertising agency to vent their feelings, whether political, religious, or otherwise.

"With the advent of personal computers, nearly everyone literally had his own print shop. People started making posters promoting every subject known to man. I still have to laugh at some of the odd-ball subjects, but a couple of real winners come to mind that really took off.

"Perhaps, Mr. Williams, you have seen some of them on display in store windows around town. It seems the two that have gained nation-wide fame are the ones that deal with juvenile crime and abortion. The one that really jumps out at you is displayed in many store windows and proclaims that '*Children Brought Up in Sunday School are Seldom Brought Up in Court.*' It was claimed that, although it was hard to prove the connection, statistics showed an actual decline in the juvenile crime rate.

"The other poster that attracted much attention also appeared in many businesses, especially drug stores, and announced: '*We Prescribe the Adoption Option.*' Again, there was no way to prove that it resulted in a decrease in the number of abortions, but pharmacists did report a substantial rise in the number of inquiries as to alternatives and information about adoption agencies.

"Incidentally as an aside, I might add that while these signs were slowly added to merchant's windows in the beginning of the program, once Paul Harvey heard about it and mentioned them on the air, supply couldn't meet the demand. The concepts spread like wild fire. You might be happy to know that while you were asleep, a national Media Museum was established just outside of Pittsburgh, Pennsylvania. That site was chosen as it was the home of the first commercial radio station in America, KDKA, which, I believe, started broadcasting exactly one hundred years ago in 1920. It is fascinating, especially to the older generations that can remember such scribes as Walter Winchell and even Hedda Hopper. At the beautifully landscaped entrance, the place of honor, in the form of a life size statue, is occupied by non other than Paul Harvey and, yes, he is behind a microphone.

"Mr. Williams, I'm sure you recall *Roe v. Wade* in your day. Well, it was never overturned, per se, but the Supreme Court did, more or less, toss the issue back to the respective states. Most folks were not aware that prior to *Roe v. Wade*, seventy-five percent of America's population lived within a hundred miles of where they could obtain a legal abortion. The nine folks in the black robes finally concluded it was not right for them to force states in the Bible Belt to allow the murder of the unborn or, conversely, tell the liberal states they are forbidden to allow such a practice. To former President Bush's credit, he succeeded in getting legislation passed that put a stop to the so-called partial-birth abortions.

"If it hasn't been covered, I'd like to add that one of the positions that killed liberalism in this country was their stand in favor of abortion while fighting the death penalty. With that, I'll relinquish the microphone to the next speaker.

"After that, what say we take a coffee and potty break?" asked Williams. "I'd also like to take this opportunity to thank Franz Bakery for supplying the wonderful baked goods we've enjoyed for many days now."

Twenty minutes later, when the session resumed, hands shot up like rockets when Hugh asked for the next volunteer. It was impossible to ascertain which hand won the first-up contest so the professor arbitrarily selected the paw that belonged to Roger Brett. "I know, I should be choosing by the length of your respective straws, but we would be spending much of our session measuring straws and missing out on some very enlightening subjects. I had no idea there would be so many folks willing to share information."

After a short introduction, Mr. Brett launched into his subject, which could have been labeled 'Crime and Punishment.'

"Mr. Williams, do you remember about the time of your accident the great hue and cry about the high crime rate and the lack of punishment? Well, I don't know where it started, but I believe your own Clark County, across the river, may have been a leader in jail reforms.

"The powers that be in that progressive county wised up to the fact that their jail contained not just career criminals, but folks down on their luck who were just looking for a home. Could you blame them? Picture yourself out on the street—cold, wet and hungry. Didn't it make sense to toss a brick through a plate glass window and be rewarded with three hots and a cot plus medical care?

"Time has blurred my memory, so can't say whether the law wanted justice or it was a guilty conscience on their part knowing that many citizens working for minimum wages weren't living as well as some of the jail's inmates. Whatever the motivation, the prisoner's standard of living took a sudden drop and the inmate population experienced a dramatic nose-dive.

"What brought this about? It was really quite simple. The offenders were provided with bread and water for nourishment and the comfortable cots were changed into pine planks. Did this reform the petty criminals? No, but it was a safe bet their next crime was not perpetrated in Clark County.

"More and more jurisdictions nationwide copied these practices and those inaugurated in Maricopa County, Arizona. Some of the punishments meted out by the sheriff of that county drew national attention such as forcing inmates to wear pink underwear.

"Another mentor in the crime and punishment sector was also a sheriff from Arizona, Clarence Dupnik of Pima County. I had the privilege of listening to an address he made to the Rotary Club of Tucson way back in April of two double aught three. As I recall, during his introductory remarks he gave his back ground in law enforcement, both with the City of Tucson and with the Pima County sheriff's office. He mentioned that he was not a politician and was not a religious fanatic but attributed the rapid rate of the increase in crime and juvenile delinquency to the fact that America took God out of our schools.

"Evidently I was not the only one he impressed that day for now, in spite of his age, he is on the lecture circuit and spreading his wisdom at civic clubs all over the nation."

"Thanks so much, Mr. Brett," responded Hugh Williams. "That's some of the most refreshing news I have heard in days." With that, a hand shot up and a feminine voice spoke to let it be known she had something to add in the field of crime and punishment.

"My name is Millie Jayne and I have attended many of these cultural exchanges but don't recall any mention of international crime.

"Back in the early part of this century, a sobbing lady from Russia appeared on the evening news one night explaining that her husband had kidnapped their children and fled to another country. He was clever enough to pick a country that refused to extradite the youngsters back to Russia. Evidently the tears she shed were not in vain as they melted the hearts of even the most hardened representatives in the United Nations and, I believe at last count, at least 168 countries have signed onto an agreement that pledges not to harbor kidnappers."

"Thank you so much Millie," remarked Professor Williams.

"Are you the *thoroughly modern Millie* we used to sing about?" Hugh thought he might get a laugh from that question, but he suddenly remembered that song was now right at 100 years old.

"As I mentioned earlier, we are apparently making the club house turn and heading down the homestretch. As you may have guessed by now, I hate committees with a passion but we do need some organization for our big finale. I'm counting on you folks to get out invitations to everyone that ever signed in at one of our sessions. We will have to rent a sizable hall and we'll no doubt have to have the affair catered.

The invites should read RSVP so we'll have a handle on what our needs will be. We will no doubt have to assess a charge to cover our out-of-pocket costs, however, in my day, we were frequently able to persuade suppliers such as wineries to donate product.

"I have noticed some in the audience who have probably never missed a single session and who were diligently taking notes every day. Tonight, I would like to have you make a list of any subjects you wish we had covered and tomorrow we will attempt to formulate the program for the big finale. With that, see ya' all tomorrow."

CHAPTER 24

As the students traipsed in the next morning, Hugh was reminded of an old song from his day, "*Laughing on the Outside, Crying on the Inside*," as many in the audience no doubt had mixed emotions. They dearly loved each session but realized this may well be the next to the last one.

"So how are we coming with our grandiose plans?" asked Hugh, once the thundering herd with coffee and pastry in hand, finally settled down. With that, a staff member announced he had contacted the local head of his union and they volunteered the use of their facilities that were made to order for the function planned. They did insist on a union bartender drawing the wine and beer, even if it was on a volunteer basis.

"Speaking of unions, I believe that is one subject we never covered during all of our confabs. Having belonged to the Brotherhood of Railway Clerks and later the Teamsters plus working many years in management, I have always been ambivalent toward unions. I do feel they had never been given their due for saving America from communism way back in the thirties when it was even fashionable to subscribe to socialism.

"Little did Karl Marx imagine, way back in about 1848, that the working stiff would someday own his own home, his own transportation known as an a automobile and indeed a life-style and standard of living that greatly exceeded that of the very rich of his day. We must give credit to the unions for giving workers a good reason not to succumb to the temptations dangled before them by the socialists during the depths of the depression.

"Unfortunately, some unions got too greedy and that coupled with a few bad apples in high union offices, left a bad taste in some folks' mouths. At the time of my accident, I believe union membership had slipped to something like about thirteen million. Oooops, sorry I got off track there for a moment. Back to the issues at hand—has anyone come up with some subjects we should have covered or they would like to see covered? "As it appears as though nobody seems to want to go first, let me throw out the first pitch…I would like to see us engage in a dialogue entitled: Where are they now? By that I mean, where are the leading lights of my day, politicians, writers, talk show moderators and the like?" That question must have struck a nerve as myriad hands reached for the sky. It became almost a shouting match but the apparent winner was Deanna DeBrandt.

"If it pleases the professor and the others in the class, I would like to elucidate on the subject of 'Where are they now?'

"Mr. Williams, I'm sure you recall Rush Limbaugh long before your skiing accident. In spite of the many pressures brought to bear for him to run for public office, true to his word, he steadfastly refused. He did, however, do the next best thing. He is now White House Chief of Staff and personal presidential advisor.

"One of the gentlemen that sat in for Rush's radio show occasionally was a brilliant man by the name of Tony Snow. Talk about an opinion molder, that man would have won the blue ribbon. Unfortunately, the Good Lord needed him more than America and we were robbed of his talented tongue way too prematurely. Other talk show hosts, especially those of the conservative persuasion, now enjoy the status of writers and political advisors. As cream rises to the top, so did such moderators as Tom Sullivan.

"Do you remember Bill O'Reilly of Fox News? Perhaps not, as he was just really starting to blossom during your last years before your long nap. Perhaps you remember him as a newscaster on a local TV station here in Portland. I think the 2000 presidential election with the hanging chads really brought out the best in him. If you have been reading the current news, you no doubt are aware that he is now our Secretary of State. A tie or a close second would have to go to Sean Hannity whom followed Mr. O'Reilly's show on Fox News.

"I believe that during our private conversation this morning you mentioned that you were a friend of Jennifer Dunn, a former Congresswoman from your state of Washington. She did wonders for her gender. Many of us were saddened when we couldn't convince her to seek even higher office.

"You may remember that when Bob Dole was a candidate, some folks were only half kidding when they jokingly proclaimed that his lovely wife, Elizabeth should have been the candidate. Well, it was also said that perhaps Jennifer Dunn would have *headed up* a GOP ticket but, tragically, God called her upstairs way too soon.

"Oops, how could I forget Dr. Laura Schlessinger? While I'm discussing famous ladies, I have to give her credit, for through her radio talk show and her books, she was single-handedly responsible for saving the institution of marriage as we have known it for millenniums.

"A former mayor of San Diego, Roger Hedgecock, hosted a talk show and eventually ended up as an advisor to the governor in Sacramento and not a minute too soon as California had elected a man who was in way over his head and he could have bankrupted the state. If you were to check a who's who back in D.C. today, you will find such notables as Ann Coulter and Michael Savage. They really paid their dues by alerting America to the subtle ways we were being brainwashed. What a tragedy that an up and coming author by the name of Barbara Olson perished in the hi-jacked plane that struck the Pentagon back in 2001. She should have been posthumously honored for her book, *The Final Days*, which was published after her death. Another leading light for the conservative cause was Mark Levin and our own Lars Larson from KXL, here in Portland didn't have to take a back seat to anyone, especially when it came to local politics. Victoria Taft kept the local city hall clowns not only on their feet, she had them tap dancing and to a different tune.......hers.

"Another part-time talk show host, also with the name of Williams—Walter E.Williams—ended up splitting his time between his university teaching position and that of chief advisor in the Department of Commerce. He could have been Secretary of that Department, but he laughingly declined saying he could remember what happened to the last black Secretary of Commerce. As it turned out, those folks made wise decisions without projecting the huge profiles they would have presented as top dogs.

"They say that three's a charm, so I can't leave out Bob Williams who heads up *Evergreen Freedom Foundation* up in Olympia in our neighbor to the north. When he talks, everybody, even liberals, listen.

"One of the most notable personalities from your day, Hugh, was Oprah Winfrey. Would you believe she is now our Ambassador to The United Nations? While her warm personality is making many friends for America, she can wield a large stick. Indeed, when she spoke before that world group, in her introductory speech, she told them where the bear defecated in the buckwheat. She announced that she had removed the sign that America's ambassadors had worn on their backsides for decades that read 'Kick Me.' She figured that if the United States was paying about one fourth of the UN's budget, we should have a lot more to say about the manner in which it is spent.

'I didn't think Oprah was old enough to remember a popular song from way back in the fifties called the '*Dark Town Poker Club*,' but she quoted from it when she said, 'Now I'm coming into this game with some rules you *must* follow when you play.' The whole country held its breath, but it worked. America is still not loved by all, but that day Oprah gained for us a lot of respect.

"I would be remiss if I didn't include characters that had a negative effect on America. Perhaps the most notable was Jesse Jackson. Back in the early part of this century, even the media started ignoring him and many newspapers refused to put the title of Reverend before his name. He was an absolute disgrace to his race and did more to sabotage what Martin Luther King, Jr. had done for minorities than anyone else, even those few avowed racists that remained in America. It seemed that this guy just wouldn't go away. Then one day, instead of picking on the working poor in our country, the IRS finally decided to crack down on folks who hid behind 'charities' and bilk the honest taxpayers. They came down hard on Jesse and his Rainbow Coalition.

"You know they say that bad news travels fast and the advent of the PC really speeded up the process. When some of the facts regarding certain politicians hit the Internet, that was all she wrote. The black man was no longer a poor downtrodden human being following a mule. They are educated, many with college degrees and will no longer accept politicians at face value. When they learned that Jesse Jackson had stood on the tarmac of the airport in Havana and with his arm around Castro, proclaimed, '*Viva Castro, viva la revolucion, viva Che Guevarra,*' that did it. His stock really plunged.

Thank God for the enlightened work of personalities such as Larry Elder who helped to reeducate his race through both his broadcasts and his books.

"It was a long time coming, but minorities in America finally wised up to the fact they were actually being held in indentured servitude by the party that was pretending to have their welfare at heart. I might add that Julian Bond was not winning any popularity contests either."

"Thanks so much, Deanna. I'm sure you probably reminded many of us of others that could shed a lot more light on more folks that had a large influence on our lives during the last twenty years. However, the constraints of time preclude us from partaking of the wisdom of everyone in attendance. Perhaps we should contact one of the colleges and convince them they should offer a course entitled 'Gems of the Generations' and insisting that at least four generations be represented in the class. I have discovered that each generation can teach others something, although I keep harking back to the subject of music.

"And, oh yes, Deanna, I do remember Bill O'Reilly as he had already made a name for himself and took Fox News to the number one spot of all the networks. If my memory hasn't failed me, I recall that one of the rungs on his ladder of success was the stint he did here in Portland.

He became to TV what Rush was to radio. These two were probably the two biggest reasons why the liberals were unable to offer alternative programming. Try as they might, even with a cadre of Hollywood stars, they just didn't seem to get the message and that was: to succeed, you had to *have* a message. I think what really sacked their bats was the fact that news magazines that had led in circulation for generations were suddenly playing second fiddle to publications such as *Insight* published by the Washington Times along with the granddaddy of conservatism, *Human Events*. I still wonder why it took so long for *Imprimis* to gain the respect it so richly deserved.

"You alluded to the fact that bad news travels fast and I couldn't help but be reminded of a joke that was popular in Russia back in the nineties. I would keep pretending I hadn't heard it and laugh each time it was repeated. They would ask me to name the three fastest means of communication and when I answered in the negative, they would respond: Telephone, telegraph and tell a woman.

"All right, have we decided what our closing subjects will be? Who headed up that committee?"

A gentleman arose and introduced himself as Thomas Brady.

"Yes, professor, we have narrowed it down to just a few, but at the top of the list are wars and hunger. We felt that of all the questions you posed at the start of our 'semester,' these perhaps received short shrift. We have a couple of highly-qualified people who will make our banquet something to write home about. Invitations have been extended to everybody and his dog, including many elected officials such as a couple of mayors and governors."

CHAPTER 25

The big day found the Resurrection Retirement Resort a virtual ghost town as most of the inhabitants, and indeed, it seemed like half the staff had migrated down to the union hall. Some to help with everything from cleaning to decorating and some just to assure themselves of a front row seat for the 'really big shew' as Ed Sullivan used to say way back in the sixties. Thanks to a lot of volunteers— some with pickup trucks—even those confined to wheelchairs—were not denied the opportunity to enjoy the big farewell doings.

If they thought the clinking of coffee cups was loud during the many coffee klatches, they really got an earful when the sound of the glassware reached about a hundred decibels. Perhaps it was because beer and wine was not readily available back at Resurrection that some of the residents were apparently making up for lost time.

The local eateries came through like champs and really outdid themselves by serving shrimp cocktails and such delicacies as lobster and escargot. This was followed by a choice of entrees from among fish, fowl, beef and pork. The program mentioned that even a special vegetarian gourmet meal was available upon request. When the volunteer kitchen crew saw how much their services were appreciated by the senior citizens, some even offered to bring hors d'oeuvres to the home and conduct an occasional bingo game and the like.

"Good evening, ladies and gentlemen," was the opening remark by the 'Professor.' "For the benefit of those whom I have never had the pleasure of meeting, my name is Hugh Williams, sometimes referred to as a modern Rip Van Winkle. For those of you who are tired of looking at my homely face, all I can say is…you lose again and you're stuck with me, at least for a few minutes. Then our MC for the evening will introduce the dignitaries attending this evening's function, which in turn will be followed by tonight's program. It gives me a great deal of pleasure to introduce to you our MC for the evening, Ms. Josephine Suell." He let out a loud chuckle and then asked, "fooled you didn't I? Isn't it strange how even in this enlightened age we somehow still think that MC stands for Master of Ceremonies? Well, tonight, it stands for Mistress of Ceremonies."

"Thank you so much, Mr. Williams. It is indeed a pleasure to serve in that capacity this evening. While I did not attend the entire course, I hope you will give me an incomplete and not an F. I did sit in on enough of the lectures to get the feel of the wonderful program you inaugurated at Resurrection. You're going to hate me as I lost the notes you gave me that had all those wonderful things I'm supposed to say about you. Just kidding, your past speaks for itself and just the fact that your 'students' want to take more courses with you at the helm says more than any description I might dream up."

"What you lost my notes?" came a response from Hugh.

"Just for that, you all have to endure one of my favorite jokes. Some of you may recall that one of my avocations is stand-up comedy and every subject mentioned reminds me of a story.

"Little Johnny asked his mother one day, 'Mommy how old are you?' His mother responded, 'Johnny, you never ask a lady her age.' The next day, Johnny asked her, 'Mommy, how much do you weigh?' Johnny's mother was beginning to lose patience and retorted, 'Son, that is even worse than asking a lady her age.' A couple of days later, little Johnny was rifling through his mother's purse and after seeing her driver's license confronted his mother. 'Mommy, I know how old you are, you're thirty-two and I know how much you weigh, it's 128 pounds.' Before his mother could respond, Johnny added; 'and I know why daddy left you, it's because you got an F in sex.'"

"Don't quit your day job," was all the wisdom the MC could muster after this unscheduled interruption to the evening's program.

"Tonight it is my pleasure to introduce the head table which consists of, from my right to my left, the Honorable Governor of Oregon, the Honorable Mayor of Portland, the Honorable Mayor of Vancouver and last but not least, the Honorable Governor of Washington. No, there is no significance to the fact one governor is on my extreme right and the other on my extreme left."

While the laughter was dying down, a note was passed to the MC, which she quickly read and immediately apologized as she announced that the Mayor of Gresham had somehow snuck into the crowd almost unnoticed. "I'm sorry, but I don't recall seeing your name on the RSVP response list and I would certainly feel remiss if I overlooked it."

"Don't apologize," responded the mayor…"It was my fault for not advising you that I planned to attend. It was only at the last minute my calendar gave me this window so I could be here."

After the introductions, Josephine gave a thumbnail sketch of the history of the daily get-together and how the generations had related to one another. It was felt that this was needed as many of the guests had never attended *any* of the classes but knew about the sessions due to so much publicity. "Had we known this function was going to be so popular, we would have sold tickets. I'm only disappointed that I don't have the popcorn concession.

"For the benefit of newcomers, I must advise you that a few days ago the participants appointed a committee and took a poll as to what subjects were to be covered at this 'graduation' banquet. As shown in your programs, we have a couple of speakers prepared to bring Hugh Williams up to date on the subjects of war and world hunger. With that, it gives me a great deal of pleasure to introduce and present Bart Douglas, an attorney who has made quite a study of the subject of war. He had minored in psychology and sociology in college and the study of the phenomenon of war became his avocation. Mr. Douglas, if you please."

"Thank you, Ms. Suell. I have read some notes and viewed some tapes of previous sessions of this group, so I'm certainly *not* going to pawn myself off as an expert. I understand, Mr. Williams, you were brought up to speed on the war on terrorism. Funny, how so many of the members of the UN did not want to help Iraq rid herself of a Hitler-like dictator, but after Uncle Sam with the aid of the UK , Canada, Poland and others got the job done, every chicken nation wanted to be there for the spoils. To our credit, America took those spoils, which consisted mostly of oil, and used them to forge a democratically elected government that became the showplace of the Middle East. Would you believe many of her neighbors are now interested in the same climate for their people? This dangling carrot, coupled with threats from a now-*more*-united United Nations, had a great deal to do with the decline in the number of terrorist attacks.

"About the same time, another rogue nation, by the name of North Korea, started to feel her oats and began to put out feelers, bragging about her nuclear capabilities. For once, I was proud of the UN. I couldn't believe that Russia, China, South Korea, Japan and the United States acted in unison and, in so many words, advised North Korea that should she wave the nuclear sabre in the face of any other nation, she would instantly become the world's largest parking lot and glow in the dark. It's amazing, the sudden change of attitude.

"It took all those years for the world to learn that together, through strength, peace could be achieved, instead of badmouthing America and then sending us the bill. The U.N. sent the same message to all its members. It said, in no uncertain terms, that any country that wanted to try her luck against the newly formed 'Peaceful Nuclear or Else Club,' would be treated the same way as one would treat a small child with a gun; they would disarm him. It was the first time I'd heard any discussion of a pre-emptive strike.

"All my life, I had wondered why America hadn't sent the same message to Uncle Joe Stalin, back in 1948 when the Russians block-aded Berlin. At that time, we were the only nation with an A-bomb and had we confronted the Kremlin, chances are the Korean War and Vietnam conflict would have never happened. Evidently America was tired of war and tried to buy peace with her wealth with such things as the Marshall plan. You know they say that hindsight is 20/20 but what a pity we became too soon old and too late smart and never used our strength to keep the peace. I hope I didn't sound too political and I thank you for your kind attention."

Professor Williams led the applause.

"Thank you, Mr. Douglas. I didn't realize that an attorney could cover such a subject and be so succinct. Sorry, Madam MC, I didn't mean to usurp your duties but my watch tells me we are running a little ahead of schedule so with your kind permission, I'd like to get my last two cents worth in." "Fine, Mr. Williams, if you want to insert a 'quickie' subject, and the guests don't mind, we'd probably love to hear your last 'lecture.'"

"Those of you who attended the last session will recall that we more or less took a vote on the last two subjects to be discussed and I'm happy with the results, but if there are no objections, I'd like to say that the 'Where are they now?' subject made me want to ask: What ever happened to the ACLU? You may recall that we discussed it briefly during a previous class? I'll never forget how controversial they were back at the turn of the century, in fact, many of us referred to them as the American Commie Lovers Union.

"I hope that times have changed as I recall in my day the ACLU was famous, or should I say infamous, for the planks in their constitution. Back in the 90s, I did some research on that subject and couldn't believe my eyes when I discovered they believed that:

- Drugs should not be prohibited by law.
- School discipline must be strictly limited.
- Jail terms should be limited to murderers and traitors.
- The Constitution requires increased welfare spending.
- There should be no draft, even in wartime.
- No secret operations against terrorists.
- Churches and synagogues should lose their tax-exempt status.
- The First Amendment protects all pornography, including child porn.
- Rating of movies is unconstitutional.
- Prostitution should be legal.
- Homosexuals should be allowed to marry and become foster parents.
- Work-fare is unconstitutional.

"When I read those planks, I had to pinch myself and ask, 'Am I really in America? What would our founding fathers think of this sicko nonsense?' While I was still trying to comprehend that America's political climate had changed so radically as to accept such garbage, I had to adjust my frame of mind. I kept telling myself that I should overlook that platform as it came within the purview of the Freedom of Speech.

"Speaking of Freedom of Speech, just in case the public is as sue happy now as they were in my day, perhaps I should practice a little CMA, you know, cover my anatomy. Therefore, thanks to my daughter who found the information in my old files, I can say that the platform I mentioned a couple of minutes ago was not a figment of my imagination but was taken from the *Wall Street Journal* of October 3, 1988. Where is that weird organization today?"

Several hands shot up in the audience as it seemed several folks wanted to elucidate on the subject of the ACLU. The shouting match was won by Kelly Roberts.

"Like the others, I don't claim to be an expert, just a life-long conservative. I have watched that group as I have always considered them a left-wing organization and have put them in the category of far-left.

"I think what really took the crocheted bathtub was the ACLU stand toward NAMBLA—North American Man-Boy Love Association. That sick group advocated sexual relations between men and young boys. They preached that their members should infiltrate Boy Scout Troops as leaders and the like. I could not believe it when I read that the ACLU actually defended that bunch of morons when NAMBLA was sued.

"The ACLU defended every odd-ball, off-the-wall, splinter group that came down the pike. Back in aught three, they screamed like banshees because a couple of monuments in the Grand Canyon contained passages from the Bible. They kept insisting that the First Amendment called for the separation of church and state but to this day, I am still not convinced that the First Amendment contains any such provision.

"Incidents like the NAMBLA case helped to diminish ACLU's

membership and once folks were really wise to them, it was a wonder that such a group even survived. Now I am informed that in this day and age, they at least pretend to defend all political persuasions and at least give lip service to the practice of equal treatment. Now we refer to them as the Anti-Christian Liberal Union."

"Oooops," exclaimed Hugh after looking at his watch. "I'm probably stepping on someone else's toes. Back to you, Madam Mistress of Ceremonies."

"I'd say it's probably time for that old seventh inning stretch," announced Ms. Suell as she gently banged the gavel. "Be back in ten for the grand finale." During that brief recess, those at the head table didn't even get a potty break as it seemed half the audience wanted to converse with 'students,' faculty, governors, mayors and especially the 'professor.' They brought up subjects never dreamed of and, indeed, had the old rascals from Resurrection realized there was such an interest in the exchanges between the generations, they could have and would have extended the course.

When the din of about three hundred voices died down to a roar, Josephine again banged the gavel, but much louder this time. She realized that if she didn't call the session to order soon, they might be looking for a breakfast menu.

"Okay, honored guests, fellow historians, politicians, economists, attorneys, engineers, students and—whom did I leave out? It's time to listen to the one speaker we've all been wanting to hear with the subject we've all been waiting for. It is indeed a pleasure and an honor to present to you a person that we might call our valedictorian. While we *rehearsed* what I was going to say in my introduction, I think it's only fitting that we let him blow his own horn. With that, let's listen to what our retired engineer from Oregon State, Mr. John Gaston Michael has to say on the subject of world hunger."

"Thank you so much, Madam MC. After that buildup, I sincerely hope that my subject won't disappoint this fine group and I certainly hope nobody asks for a refund. Only being facetious, and as you can probably observe, I never was noted for my sense of humor. Probably, it's due, in no small part, to the human tragedies I have witnessed, all over the globe, directly attributable to hunger.

"Back in about twenty ten, there was a great hue and cry all over America for those responsible for our farm programs to either fish or get off the yacht." Some snickers from the audience actually brought a grin to the speaker's rather stern expression. "For too many years, on TV, America had seen the faces of starving children, especially in Africa, with distended bellies and flies swarming all over them.

"It was, I believe, a group of farmers from the mid-west that brought up the subject at a Grange meeting. During the open discussion portion of the meeting, one farmer stood up and asked, 'How come Uncle Sam is paying us not to grow crops and nightly we see starving children on TV? I don't know about the rest of you, but personally, I think I could sleep a lot better at night if I was *helping* a charity instead of being the recipient of charity.'

"I heard that the hall suddenly became a cacophony of 'here, here's' and gave birth to a whole new agriculture policy in America. Since that time Uncle Sam has embarked on a 'feed the hungry' program wherein instead of paying our farmers for not producing meat and grains, we purchased those commodities and shipped them to every third-world nation on earth.

"When an emergency famine reared its ugly head, we used huge cargo planes to air-lift the relief supplies. On a couple of occasions some tin-horn dictators challenged us by refusing to let us use their airspace but the fighter escorts and some well placed ordnance soon brought their threats to a screeching halt.

"Some of you may recall that early in your school 'semester' the subject of super-conductivity was alluded to. Now you'll see why that speaker graciously skipped over the ramifications of that subject which I am about to discuss. You may also recall that he briefly mentioned the fact that with the transmission lines of your day, Mr. Williams, most of the energy was lost due to friction.

"With the advent of wires capable of handling super-conductivity at room temperatures, the cost of electricity dropped dramatically. Of course to the average consumer, it meant he could afford to use electric cars. He could now heat with clean non-fossil fuels and it enabled even folks near the bottom of our economic ladder to enjoy the luxury of air-conditioning.

"The biggest reward of all was the fact that now it was economically feasible to desalinate salt water. Now, even in areas where it is so dry, one can't even raise a disturbance; the deserts are blooming. That fact, coupled with our 'feed the world program,' enabled man to achieve what he had been seeking since the dawn of history. It is indeed my pleasure to announce that for the first time in recorded history, nobody on the face of the earth will go to bed hungry tonight."

With that, the entire hall erupted into what amounted to a standing ovation and tears were streaming down many of the faces, especially Hugh's. These were tears of joy and mixed emotions, torn between the good news shared by the last speaker and the knowledge that not only was he the *last* speaker, it was the *last* class.

Hugh could only hope that somehow the 'students,' staff and guests would receive the same vision that he had been blessed with. God sat in His Heaven, looking down upon His creation and, for the first time in nearly 2,000 years,…God smiled.

Boys who helped us in Leningrad

Summer Palace of the Czars

St. Isaacs Cathedral in Leningrad

Building from which Lenin led the Revolution

Kremlin of Novgorod

Hotel Ukraina in Moscow

Author dressed conservatively in Red Square

Winnie near Lenin's tomb in Red Square

Winnie with Kremlin across the river

Churches within the Kremlin walls

St. Basil's Cathedral at end of Red Square

(Left to right) Stewardess, Winnie and Pat Nash

Siberia has flowers in spite of perma-frost

Typical privately owned garden plot

Cemetery of the Heroes in Irkutsk

Lenin had replaced the Deity in Soviet Union

Typical village in Siberia. They lost 75 years.

Colorful locomotive

More ladies selling salads, veggies, fish, etc.

One of many kiosks along the Trans-Siberian

These had to be the world's best dill pickles

Fancy dining car on last leg of journey

Train station and steamship pier in Nakhodka

231